Leigh tried to pull away from him...

"Don't!" Her voice sounded high and breathless and her self-control was slipping. "That—that isn't what I meant, and you know it. You seem to have forgotten I'm engaged to be married."

"On the contrary. But at the moment, I have more pressing matters on my mind," Martinez said huskily, his hand stroking down the sensitive curve of her spine. "*Dios*, Leigh, I had almost forgotten how beautiful you are."

He pulled her against him so that she could feel the slight roughness of his body hair grazing her skin. "Now we're on equal terms," he murmured, smiling into her eyes.

She tried to say "No," but no sound came. All she could hear was the rasp of hurried breathing—hers, she wondered insanely, or his?

SARA CRAVEN probably had the ideal upbringing for a budding writer. She grew up by the seaside in a house crammed with books, with a box of old clothes to dress up in and a swing outside in a walled garden. She produced the opening of her first book at age five and is eternally grateful to her mother for having kept a straight face. Now she has more than twenty-five novels to her credit. The author is married and has two children.

Books by Sara Craven

HARLEQUIN PRESENTS

HARLEQUIN ROMANCE

Don't miss any of our special offers. Write to us at the following address for information on our newest releases.

Harlequin Reader Service
901 Fuhrmann Blvd., P.O. Box 1397, Buffalo, NY 14240
Canadian address: P.O. Box 603,
Fort Erie, Ont. L2A 5X3

SARA CRAVEN

night of the condor

Harlequin Books

TORONTO • NEW YORK • LONDON
AMSTERDAM • PARIS • SYDNEY • HAMBURG
STOCKHOLM • ATHENS • TOKYO • MILAN

Harlequin Presents first edition December 1987
Second printing November 1987
ISBN 0-373-11032-4

Original hardcover edition published in 1987
by Mills & Boon Limited

Printed in U.S.A.

CHAPTER ONE

THE view from her hotel bedroom window would have been panoramic, except for the fog.

Leigh could hardly believe it. Only a relatively short time ago, her plane had been circling the Jorge Chavez International Airport in brilliant sunshine. She had looked down in wondering delight at the city beneath her, and the foam-capped breakers of the Pacific Ocean beyond, with the great ridge of the Andes forcing its way to the shore like a giant, clenched fist.

Now, suddenly, it was all gone. The sunshine, the view, even the feeling of excitement and exhilaration which had filled her were all muffled under a damp, dismal blanket of grey mist.

The bell-boy who had carried up her bags had shrugged philosophically. 'It is the *garua, señorita.* The curse of Lima. It comes, and when it is the will of God, it goes.'

'I see,' Leigh muttered. She wasn't sure she believed in curses, or that changes in climatic conditions were necessarily the workings of Divine Providence, but at the same time she wished the sun had kept shining a little longer. The *garua* seemed like a bad omen, she thought, then immediately chided herself for being over-fanciful.

Activity, she told herself briskly. That's what I need. Something to do.

She unlocked her cases, and started to hang her things away in the generous cupboard space provided. She smiled a little, as her hands touched the fabrics—silk, pure cotton, and the finest, softest wool—all her favourites, and most of them brand-new. Almost a trousseau—but then that was really the idea, she thought, her heart lifting.

This enforced separation from Evan had gone on quite long enough. She wasn't sure what the rules regarding the marriage of foreigners in Peru were, but Evan, she was certain, would be able to find out.

She had been disappointed when he hadn't been there to meet her at the airport, although she knew she was being unrealistic. Even supposing all the right messages had been passed along the line at all the right times, and she had been told how unlikely that was, Evan still probably wouldn't be able to drop everything at Atáyahuanco and dash to Lima to see her. She had already resigned herself to the fact that she would have to go to him instead. But if this fog was going to persist, leaving Lima would be no great hardship anyway, she told herself, grimacing.

She looked restlessly round the suite, her unpacking completed. It was comfortable, and well appointed, and she might as well make the most of it, because Atayahuanco would be the total opposite. Evan had mentioned conditions there in his letters many times, jokingly at first, then, later, with increasing bitterness and resentment. And she had felt resentful, on his behalf. Evan hadn't deserved to be sent halfway round the world to some forgotten valley in the Andes to grub about in dirt and stone.

His only sin had been to fall in love with her, Leigh Frazier, her father's only daughter, and heiress to Frazier Industries and the network of companies and interests it controlled.

And to Justin Frazier, a self-made man who was proud of his achievements, an intended son-in-law who had neither money nor a steady job was an affront.

'But that isn't his fault!' she had raged, once Evan's departure for Atayahuanco was inevitable, and only days away.

'It's not a question of fault,' her father had returned. 'I feel he should be given a chance to prove himself—see what he's made of.'

'In South America—as some cross between an archaeologist and a social worker?' she had protested.

'It's a worthwhile project,' Justin Frazier had replied tersely. 'Evan's a history graduate, and he's always had a lot to say about poverty, and the dignity of labour. Well, Atayahuanco will give him a chance to study both of them at first hand.' He paused. 'He wants work. I've given it to him.'

'There are other jobs. . .'

'There could be—if this one works out.' He stood up, a tall man with a craggy face. Evan called him formidable, and she supposed he was. 'But not yet awhile.' He put a hand on her shoulder, and his voice gentled. 'You're young, Leigh, and so is your man. You need a breathing space, both of you, before embarking on anything as serious as marriage. If you really love each other, and he's the right man for you, then a year's wait—eighteen months even—isn't going to make a radical difference.' He paused. 'Unless you doubt him—or yourself.'

Which, of course, was unanswerable, as well as unthinkable, and he knew it.

Evan had been stoically philosophical. 'It might not be too bad.' He put his arms around her, drawing her close. 'And if it convinces your father that I don't simply see you as a meal-ticket for life, it will be worth any hassle.'

'That's ridiculous,' Leigh protested hotly. 'I don't think my father remembers what it was like to be young.'

Evan grimaced slightly. 'Perhaps not, but he has the right to apply some pressure if he wants to.' He sighed. 'I feel a bit like one of those guys in the old stories who were always being sent off on quests before they could win the princess.'

She had smiled at that, in spite of her unhappiness. She had always loved those stories. 'What are you going to do—climb a glass mountain, and bring me back a golden apple?'

'Maybe I will at that. After all, Atayahuanco was once an Inca citadel, and the Incas went in for gold in a big way. Perhaps I'll find the lost treasure they hid from the Spaniards, and lay it all at your feet.' He laughed. 'Your father would really be impressed then.'

'He certainly would!' She laughed with him, but the glance she sent him was slightly troubled, just the same. 'Evan, you do realise this isn't a conventional archaeological dig you're going on? It might have started out that way, but the emphasis switched a long time ago. As well as trying to build up a picture of how the Incas lived in that particular place, the team's trying to rehabilitate the Indian families who still live there, but have lost touch with their traditional skills and lifestyle. I don't think there's any treasure-seeking going on.'

'Darling Leigh!' He kissed her. 'You sound like a brochure for Peruvian Quest. I do know all that— my God, I should, because it's been drilled into me *ad nauseam*. I'm not going to Atayahuanco with any preconceived notions about what I'm going to find there. I'm going to convince your father that I'd make the ideal son-in-law—docile, obedient, and industrious.'

Brave words, thought Leigh, as she relived the conversation, but in reality Evan had been violently shocked by the conditions in the valley. And the desperate jokiness of his early letters, outlining the squalor and hardship on the site, had soon degenerated into angry bewilderment, and a string of complaints.

His most recent letters had suggested he was near the end of his tether, and it was these which had led to her sudden decision to fly out to Peru to join him, in spite of her father's forcefully stated opposition.

But this time, Leigh had been adamant. 'We've been apart for a year. We're of age, and we're in love. We deserve a little happiness.'

She had faltered slightly when she realised Justin Frazier was not prepared to assist in any way with her arrangements.

'I'm not going to ease your path for you, Leigh,' he said flatly. 'This whole idea is madness from start to finish. I can only hope when you get to Lima and realise the problems confronting you, your own common sense will bring you home again.'

His words had lingered uneasily throughout that interminable journey, in spite of her efforts to tell herself that when she got to Peru, happiness would be hers for the taking. But now—with Evan's failure to show at the airport, the sheer impersonality of this hotel suite, and, most of all, the swirling sea mist outside—all her old doubts had returned.

Leigh gave herself a brief mental shake. She needed some practical stimulation. She supposed she should eat, but she was too strung up to be hungry. On the other hand, some coffee might be good. As she moved to the internal telephone beside the wide bed to call room service, it rang, startling her.

She lifted the receiver. 'Yes?'

'Señorita Frazier, there is a gentleman here at reception asking for you. Do you wish to come down and speak to him?'

A smile began to spread across Leigh's face. Evan, she thought, her depression lifting miraculously. She said, 'Ask him to come up here, *por favor*.'

There was a short silence, then the clerk said, 'You are certain that is what you wish, *señorita*?'

'Yes, of course,' Leigh returned with a trace of impatience. 'And will you arrange for some coffee to be sent up too.'

'At once, *señorita*.' The phone went down.

She sped to the dressing-table, and tugged a comb through her shoulder-length tawny hair so that it curved elegantly towards her neck. She renewed her lipstick hastily, wishing with irritation that she had changed from the clothes she had been travelling in. But the spare lines of the chic sand-coloured linen dress still looked relatively fresh, she decided, and after their long separation Evan, she hoped, would be too delighted to see her to be over-concerned about the finer details of her appearance.

She put up a hand and touched the gold chain she wore round her throat. She thought, I'm nervous. Nervous of seeing Evan again. But that's ridiculous. It's what I want, after all, what I came all this way for.

For one nightmare moment, she tried and failed to remember what Evan looked like, reminding herself, as panic rose inside her, that the same thing was said to happen to brides on their way to the altar.

The brisk rap on the door was a relief, cutting across the blankness in her mind. She took a deep steadying breath, as she walked across the room, and her smile was firmly back in place as she flung open the door.

She said gaily, 'Darling, you got here at last. . .' then stopped dead, because no trick of the mind could ever have turned the complete stranger confronting her into Evan.

Evan was fair, and this man was as dark as midnight—thick black hair springing back from a high forehead, a lean face, with high cheekbones, deeply tanned, the lines of nose, mouth and chin all forcefully, even harshly marked. He was tall, long-legged, and broad-shouldered, dressed in denims, with a worn leather jacket slung carelessly across one shoulder.

Leigh said sharply, 'Who are you? What do you want?'

He gave her an unsmiling look. 'It might have been wiser to have established that before inviting me to your room, Miss Frazier. Do you usually behave so recklessly in a foreign country?'

She said glacially, 'I was expecting my fiancé.'

'My regrets for your disappointment.' He neither looked nor sounded even slightly regretful. 'I presume you had some reason to believe he would meet you here?'

Leigh's chin tilted. 'May I know what business this is of yours, Mr. . . er. . .?'

'Rourke Martinez,' he said. 'And it's "Doctor", Miss Frazier.' He looked at her drily. 'I see the name is familiar to you.'

Oh, she had heard of him all right, Leigh thought faintly. Most of Evan's discontent had been centred on this man. 'Everyone defers to him,' he had written shortly after his arrival. 'He stalks round the camp behaving as if he was one of the ancient Incas with the power of life and death over us all. Even Fergus Willard, who's technically in charge, does as he tells him.'

Knowing that her instinctive reaction to his name had given her away too thoroughly to warrant a denial, she gave a slight shrug. 'I believe Evan has mentioned you, Doctor Martinez, yes.'

'I'm sure he has.' He sounded faintly amused. 'And not in any flattering terms either, unless I miss my guess. Now that my identity has been established, are you going to invite me in? Or would you prefer this interview to be conducted in one of the reception areas downstairs?'

'Arrogant bastard' had been another of Evan's descriptions, and it seemed perfectly justified, Leigh thought, her hackles rising.

Down the corridor, the lift doors opened, and a white-coated waiter emerged, with a tray of coffee. The coffee which she had ordered. And although there was nothing she wanted less than to have to invite Rourke Martinez into her suite, she could see that to object would cause unnecessary complications, and probably make her look foolish into the bargain.

She said abruptly, 'You'd better come in,' and turned back into the suite.

The waiter deposited the tray where she indicated on the table by the window, and stood waiting for the inevitable tip. Rourke Martinez provided it with a brief word in Spanish, but not before the waiter sent Leigh an infuriating leer, shared equally between herself, the open door to the inner room, and the big bed which suddenly seemed to dominate it.

She was aware she was flushing angrily, as she pulled forward a chair and sat down. 'Coffee, Doctor Martinez?'

'Black, please.' He took the cup she handed him, with a word of thanks, then leaned back in his own chair, very much at ease. Then he said quietly, 'What are you doing here, Miss Frazier? Why have you come?'

'To join my fiancé. I should have thought that was obvious.' His whole attitude needled her, making her speak more sharply than she would normally have done. 'Is it any concern of yours?'

'As he's employed on the Atayahuanco project, and I happen to be its co-director, then I'd say I was concerned,' he said grimly. 'May I ask who authorised you to come here? I certainly didn't, and nor did Doctor Willard. By the time we received notification of your arrival, it was too late to turn you back.'

'I wasn't aware you had any right to do so.' Leigh was rigid with shock and temper. She set her cup down carefully, to avoid hurling it at him.

'We have any rights in this that we choose to assume, Miss Frazier,' Rourke Martinez said almost casually. 'Our work at Atayahuanco is difficult enough, without deliberately inviting additional problems in the shape of random visitors.' His eyes skimmed her, indicating silently but unmistakably that the shape of this particular random visitor failed to impress him in any way. He went on, 'Your arrival seems to indicate one of two things—either you expect Evan Gilchrist to join you here in Lima, or that you expect to go to Atayahuanco to be with him.' He paused. 'I'm afraid that neither possibility is acceptable.'

Leigh sat up very straight in her chair. She said, 'Doctor Martinez, I don't think you realise. . .'

'Exactly who I'm talking to?' he finished for her. 'Yes, I do, Miss Frazier. I'm well aware that it's a charitable trust set up by Frazier Industries which provides most of the financing for our project. I'm also aware that you probably consider that gives you *carte blanche* to do as you wish here.' He paused again. 'Well, I'm here to tell you you're wrong, and to give you some advice.'

She smiled icily, controlling her temper with an heroic effort. 'Am I supposed to be grateful?'

'That's up to you,' he said. 'But for what it's worth, I suggest you get the next available flight back to the United Kingdom. This is no place for you, and I'm surprised your family didn't tell you so.' He gave her another assessing look. 'Or did they?'

'I happen to be an adult, Doctor Martinez,' Leigh said loudly and clearly. 'I do as I want.'

'Not,' he said, 'a particularly adult point of view. But let that pass. Is Gilchrist meeting you here?'

'Perhaps you'd like to tell me,' she said, heavily sarcastic. 'You seem to rule the roost at Atayahuanco. Have you graciously given Evan permission to meet me?'

'No.'

'No, of course not.' She stared at him defiantly. 'And now I'm supposed to confess my fault, and grovel, right?'

He shrugged. 'It would make little difference if you did. Evan Gilchrist walked off the project some forty-eight hours before we got the radio message announcing your imminent arrival.' He paused. 'Indicating that he already knew you were coming, and had gone to meet you. But, for various reasons, I wasn't convinced.'

Leigh's mouth was dry. She picked up the cooling coffee, and drank some of it. At last she said, 'He—

he didn't know I was coming. I didn't mention it in my last letter. It was a spur-of-the-moment decision. . .' She was silent for a moment. 'Did he give no idea where he was going?'

'We had no idea he was even leaving,' Rourke Martinez told her. 'He took some provisions and a mule, and vanished in the night. There was no need to have done that, no matter how much he hated Atayahuanco and everything connected with it. If he'd given some indication that he wanted out, he could have flown out on the supply helicopter with me yesterday.' He sent her a lightning glance. 'He wasn't that much of an asset.'

She flushed again. 'Of course, you would say that. I'm sorry Evan's best was never good enough for your exacting standards, Doctor Martinez.'

'Is that what he told you?' He sounded amused again. 'I wasn't aware we'd ever seen his best, but it was difficult to look beyond the outsize chip he had on his shoulder.'

She glared at him. Other phrases of Evan's were coming back to her: 'Intolerant swine' and 'a real slave-driver'. She could believe all of them. 'Have you made any attempt to find him? Sent out a search-party?'

'He's not a child, Miss Frazier.' What curious eyes he had, she thought irrelevantly. Deeply set beneath strongly arched black brows, they were a strange colour between brown and gold almost like topaz. Eyes like a jungle cat's, she thought with a little inward shiver.

Rourke Martinez went on, 'He knows what the dangers are, or he should do by now. He's been warned often enough—about all kinds of things.'

She looked at him incredulously. 'And on the strength of that, you're prepared just to—write him off?'

'Your fiancé seems to have a strong sense of self-preservation,'he said rather drily. 'I suspect he'll need it. In the mean time the best thing you can do is get back to the U.K. and wait for the eventual happy reunion there.'

The coffee tasted bitter, and she slammed her cup back into its saucer.

'Thanks, but no, thanks,' she said grittily. 'Evan is missing, and I've no intention of going tamely back to Britain while such a situation continues. Even if you're not sufficiently concerned about your staff to worry about his safety, I am, and I'm coming up to Atayahuanco right away to instigate some kind of search. Please be good enough to make the necessary arrangements.'

He actually had the gall to laugh.

'Thus speaks the autocrat,' he said mockingly. 'I expect you're a riot on your home ground, Miss Frazier, keeping everyone on the run. But not here. Here, you have no authority.' He paused. 'Short of marching you to the airport, and actually putting you on the plane, I can't force you out, of course.'

'I'm glad you appreciate that!'

'But I'm wondering what you appreciate.' The topaz eyes narrowed thoughtfully. 'I have to warn you, Miss Frazier, for your family's sake, if not your own, that Lima is not a safe city for a girl on her own, especially when the girl's a spectacular-looking *gringa* like yourself.' His gaze rested on the small gold hoops in her ears, the heavy links of her necklace, her watch on its slender bracelet. 'And one so evidently blessed with this world's goods too.'

'I don't need your warnings,' Leigh flashed. 'And if your peculiar remarks were intended as some kind of compliment, I can do without that too!'

'No compliment, merely an observation.' Shrugging, he pushed back his chair, and got to his feet. 'Well, stay here in Lima, if you're really so determined, but remain in the vicinity of the hotel, if you have any sense. No doubt Daddy will send some minion to bail you out, if you really get into trouble. You're not my responsibility, thank God.'

'You utter bastard,' Leigh said unevenly.

'And harsh words don't impress me either,' he said coolly. 'Did no one ever wash your mouth out with soap when you were a child, Miss Frazier, because if not they missed a golden opportunity. And a sound hiding applied to your pampered backside wouldn't come amiss either. What a pity Gilchrist isn't man enough to administer it!'

'How dare you,' Leigh was almost choking, 'speak to me—speak about Evan like that. . .'

He laughed. 'Why, are you going to tell me I'm not fit to lick his shoes, or some other cliché like that? Well, keep your illusions, Miss Frazier. If your wandering boy should wander back in our direction, I promise I'll scoop him up and deliver him to you here. You're entirely welcome to each other.'

She was trembling, her hands balled into impotents fists at her sides.

'Get out of here! Get out of here now!'

'Gladly,' he said. 'Now that I've made the situation clear to you once and for all.'

'Oh, you have,' she said icily. 'And now I'll make something clear to you—Doctor Martinez. When I get back to England, I'm going to tell my father every detail of your behaviour—raisesome questionsabout

whether you're a fit person to be in charge of the
Atayahuanco project at all, in fact. You seem to be
totally lacking in consideration and—and compassion!'

Rourke Martinez shrugged. 'Try it,' he advised
shortly, 'and see how far it gets you. Your father's no
fool, and in spite of your brave, independent words,
it's my guess that you're out here against his wishes
also. So don't blame me if he doesn't share your sense
of outrage. Here, Miss Frazier, you are not the centre
of the universe, and your father might even be grateful that someone's pointed this out to you at last.'

The topaz eyes travelled over her in one last sear-
ing look, then he walked to the door and went out.

She wanted to scream, Leigh realised incredulously. She wanted to lie down and drum her heels on
the carpet, and yell until she was hoarse.

She couldn't believe what had happened. This
man—a stranger—had treated her as if she were of
no account.

And it was infuriating that he had homed in on her
battle of wills with her father. She found herself wondering if Justin had contacted Peruvian Quest, the
umbrella organisation under which the Atayahuanco project was sheltered, and requested they
make things as difficult as possible for her. He was
quite capable of it, she thought furiously.

She walked into the bedroom and threw herself
across the bed, staring into space.

She had handled that confrontation badly, she
knew, but learning of Evan's disappearance like that
had thrown her completely.

Her heart ached for Evan. She realised she hadn't
fully comprehended the problems and difficulties he
had encountered at Atayahuanco, or the depth of his

wretchedness, but meeting Rourke Martinez had made a great deal clear to her.

He had obviously realised that Evan was less than wholehearted about the project, and resented having him foisted on to it. But that wasn't Evan's fault, she thought angrily. If anyone was to blame, it was her father, who should have known he was asking the impossible.

And now Evan was heaven knows where with a mule and a few supplies. He could be lost. He could be injured, she thought, biting her lip savagely, as a pang of fear tore through her. He must have been really desperate to have taken such a risk, because none of his letters had expressed the slightest interest in exploring the hostile terrain around him.

That was, of course, if Evan had really gone off at all. She sat up abruptly. After all, she only had that abominable swine's word for it, and who was to say he wasn't simply following her father's instructions to deter her.

Well, if her father thought she was going tamely back to Britain with her tail between her legs, he was mistaken. Come hell or high water, she was going to get to Atayahuanco somehow. She was going to check primarily whether Evan had really disappeared, and if so, to insist on a full-scale effort to find him.

Her lips curved in a brief cat-like smile. After all, Rourke Martinez was not the only arbiter on the project. There was Fergus Willard too. The Frazier name was bound to count for something with him. And if she managed to get his permission to make the trip to Atayahuanco, there would be nothing the Martinez man could do about it.

Or she could simply arrive there, she thought. It wouldn't be an easy trip, but she couldn't imagine she would be turned away once she had managed the journey.

She gave a determined nod. Tomorrow she would go to the Peruvian Quest offices and make radio contact with Fergus Willard. Once she had won him over, it would just be a question of hiring the best guide, and the best transport her money could obtain.

She squared her shoulders. But if she had to fight every battle alone, then she would do so. And Rourke Martinez—or anyone else for that matter—would not defeat her.

She swallowed suddenly, remembering with painful clarity those last contemptuous words he had flung at her.

I'll make him sorry, she vowed silently. I'll make him sorry he was ever born!

CHAPTER TWO

THE Peruvian Quest offices lay in a quiet side street.

Leigh stood for a moment, watching the cab which had brought her there drive off. She was sure she had been overcharged for such a comparatively modest journey, but there had been no meter in the cab for her to check with. No meter, and very little else that worked either, she thought with a kind of desperate hilarity, but most of the cabs she had seen cruising around had been in the same ramshackle state.

She wished she had taken up the hotel's offer to hire a car for her. It would surely have been in better condition, and maybe the driver wouldn't have looked like a brigand either, she thought with a slight shiver.

More than once, she had caught him staring insolently at her in his mirror, and he had tossed a couple of remarks at her which she hadn't been able to understand, but which instinct warned her were of a frankly sexual nature.

Last night, in the hotel dining-room, she had been openly stared at as she tried to eat her meal, and one man from a party of four near the door had tried to accost her as she left. She had shaken him off with a blazing look, and gone straight to her room, abandoning any notion of seeing what facilities the hotel had to offer during the evenings.

Under the circumstances, she had slept quite well, but today she was aware of a slight persistent headache, no doubt a legacy from her long plane trip.

The *garua* still held the city in its clammy grip too, which was disappointing, and although it was very humid, she was beginning to wish she had brought some warmer clothes.

Leigh walked across the uneven paving-stones and tried the heavy outer door of the building. It opened at once, and she found herself in a narrow passage facing an old-fashioned lift. On her right was a rudimentary reception counter surmounted by a grille with an ornate bellpush. She rang and waited, but no one came, and after a brief hesitation, she decided to trust herself to the lift.

Gingerly, she closed the gate and pressed the button. The lift seemed to stir and shake itself like a grumpy animal being poked with a stick, then with a heart-stopping lurch it began its upward journey.

It stopped equally abruptly, nearly throwing her off balance, but she seemed to have arrived at the first floor, so she supposed she had to be grateful for small mercies.

The narrow passage seemed a facsimile of the one downstairs, except that the reception area had been replaced by a pair of double doors. It was plainly the sole option, so she knocked briefly and walked in.

She stopped dead. Just for a moment, it seemed as if the door led nowhere, and she had fallen off the edge of the world. Then she realised that what was confronting her was a gigantic aerial photograph of part of the Andes range. She caught her breath as she studied it. Savagely sculpted peaks reared towards the pale sky, intersected by gorges, and swooping down to the unimaginable depths of chasms where slender rivers ran. Some of the most inhospitable terrain on earth, she had heard it said, and Evan—her Evan—was out there somewhere—alone.

She supposed Atayahuanco was somewhere in the photograph, hidden in the indigo shade of one of those deep valleys, and the realisation of what was facing her made her feel suddenly nauseated.

It wouldn't have taken much to persuade her to forget the whole thing, she thought with a shudder. She was no climber. In fact she was hardly the outdoor type at all. And neither was Evan, she reminded herself.

She closed her eyes momentarily, taking a grip on herself. She loved Evan. She had endured their separation, and it would take more than a little physical hardship to keep him from her now.

She heard a polite cough, and opened her eyes to find a young woman neatly dressed in a dark skirt and white blouse standing looking at her enquiringly.

Leigh marshalled one of her few Spanish phrases. *'Habla usted Inglés?'* she asked hopefully, and was rewarded by a nod and a smile.

'I speak it well. How may I help you, *señorita*?'

Leigh decided not to beat about the bush. She said, 'I understand you're in radio contact with the camp at Atayahuanco. I was wondering if I could send a message through.'

The girl looked puzzled. 'There is no radio here, *señorita*. We have another office in Cuzco, and all messages go from there. But the use of the radio is—restricted, I think.'

'I'm sure it is.' Leigh's own smile didn't slip. 'But you see, I need to contact Doctor Willard urgently, and I don't know any other way of doing it.'

The girl's face cleared. 'Doctor Willard? Ah, but that is not possible, *señorita*. Doctor Willard is ill with a fever. The camp is under the direction of Doctor

Martinez, and he is here in Lima at this time. You
may speak with him directly.'

Leigh groaned inwardly. 'Oh, I don't think there's
any need for that,' she said, trying to sound casual.
'Actually, I was hoping to go to the camp, and I just
wanted to warn someone that I was on my way, that's
all.'

The girl gaped at her. 'Go—up to Atayahuanco?'
She shook her head. 'Impossible.'

'Hardly,' said Leigh with determined amiability.
'This—Doctor Martinez seems to manage it.' She
remembered something he'd said. 'How do supplies
go in? Isn't there a helicopter, or something?'

'*Sí,señorita*. But this month it has already made its
trip.'

'Then what do you suggest?' Leigh asked.

The girl shrugged. 'Me, I would not go,' she said
with total seriousness.

Leigh held on to her temper. 'Doctor Martinez—
how will he travel?'

The girl moved her shoulders again with growing
reluctance. 'From Cuzco, *señorita,* he goes by jeep,
and later by mule. But then,' she added, a disturbingly dreamy expression crossing her face, 'Doctor
Martinez is a man, and very strong, and altogether
unafraid.'

'And when he needs to cross a river, I suppose he
walks on water,' muttered Leigh. She saw the other
girl looked astonished, and waved a dismissive hand.
'Oh, let it pass.' Her mind was moving rapidly,
weighing the various possibilities, and realising with
increasing foreboding that the most direct route to
Atayahuanco, little though she might relish it, lay in
the company of the loathsome Martinez man.

And, of course, he's so likely to welcome me as a
travelling companion, she thought despondently. If

I'd known, I might have been nicer to the pig.

As it was, she seemed to have burned her boats pretty comprehensively where he was concerned.

Or had she?

She gritted her teeth. 'Is Doctor Martinez here?'

The girl glanced at her watch. 'He is expected, *señorita,* but when it is impossible to say, you understand.'

'Well, I'll wait for a while, if that's all right.'

'As you wish.' The girl indicated a high-backed chair near the window, and offered coffee which Leigh declined. She withdrew then to some inner office, and Leigh could hear the sound of a typewriter through the closed door.

By the time an hour and a half had passed, she felt she could have drawn the aerial photograph from memory, and answered questions on it too.

But she had had time to plan the next stage in her campaign.

Bitter as gall though it was, she was going to have to make some kind of peace with Rourke Martinez.

She shouldn't have allowed his overt hostility to get to her, she thought. She should have realised he could be useful and set out to charm him from the outset. She knew, without particular vanity, that she could have done it. She had been helping her shy mother to entertain important business clients for years, and they had not always been easy to deal with either. Yet she had invariably managed, and more than managed.

'Leigh could charm birds from trees,' Justin Frazier was wont to say proudly.

Well, she would just have to charm Rourke Martinez, she thought calmly. It could be done. Even while he had been slagging her off, he had been aware of her as a woman. She knew that, and at the time it had simply fuelled her resentment of him, but now, she acknowledged, she could turn it to her advantage maybe.

She would have to apologise sweetly, she thought, grinding her teeth. Tell him helplessly that jet-lag always affected her temper. She would have to flatter him, of course. No man with his brand of dynamic good looks could be without his share of sexual vanity. It might even be—amusing to let him fancy her a little. To let him think she could be—interested herself.

She had done it before, she thought with a little inward giggle. There wasn't a man alive who couldn't be conned into thinking he was irresistible.

She would have to be discreet about it, of course. The journey to Atayahuanco would be fraught enough without having to fight off unwanted advances from her guide.

With new determination, she knocked at the door of the inner office. It opened almost at once, and the girl looked at her enquiringly.

'*Si, señorita?* You are having a long wait, I think.'

'I think so too,' Leigh said briskly. 'It might be better to leave Doctor Martinez a note, if you can give me a sheet of paper and an envelope.'

The note took a lot of thinking about. She wanted it to sound reasonably enticing, without actually grovelling to the creature.

'Dear Doctor Martinez,' she wrote at last, 'I feel we got off on the wrong foot yesterday. May I make amends by inviting you to have dinner with me at my hotel either tonight or tomorrow? I expect to be out for the rest of the day, but a message left at reception will be quite sufficient.' She added, 'Sincerely yours' and her signature, and looked at her handiwork with satisfaction. That should bring him, if only out of curiosity.

And by the time dinner was over, she would have him eating out of her hand, she thought, smiling to herself, sealing the envelope as if she were sealing his fate with it.

Leigh could not have said she thoroughly enjoyed her sightseeing that day. Armed with a guide book, she dutifully toured the Plaza de Armes, stared into the swirling waters of the Rimac from the Bridge of Stones, and recoiled, shuddering, from the mummified remains of the great *conquistador* Francisco Pizarro, preserved ghoulishly in a glass case in the Cathedral.

She wasn't sure she approved of Pizarro. Everything she had ever read about the Inca civilisation suggested it had worked perfectly well without outside interference. But the gold which they took so much for granted had lured the conquerors and plunderers from the Old World, and the Spaniards had overthrown the Inca Atahualpa by a trick, then held him to ransom. But the riches of his kingdom, which his bewildered people had brought in load after weary load, were not enough to save him. Pizarro, having sworn not one drop of his blood should be spilled, kept his word by having the Inca strangled.

It was not, Leigh thought with distaste, an uplifting story, and it seemed only fitting that a few years later Pizarro should have been betrayed and murdered by his own men.

But her mind wasn't really on Peru's savage history. Over and over again, she found herself thinking about Rourke Martinez, trying to gauge his reaction to her note.

She supposed his most likely response would be to ignore her completely. But I'll worry about that when it happens, she thought.

And much as she hated to admit it, she was beginning to realise that Lima might not be a safe city for a woman on her own. She was attracting all kinds of unwelcome attention. She could deal with the normal range of wolf whistles and goodhumoured sexual innuendo, but the kind of *macho* aggression her slender fairness seemed to be inciting was altogether outside her scope. Over-loud remarks accompanied by blatantly lecherous gestures, made her face burn, and she decided to abandon her plan to visit some of the city's museums, almost running the remaining blocks back to her hotel.

To her amazement, when she asked without much hope if there were any messages, the clerk handed her a folded paper.

'Dear Miss Frazier,' his letter read, 'Your olive branch is accepted. I'm afraid tonight is the only night I can manage, as my time in Lima is strictly limited. Shall we say eight o'clock?' His signature was as uncompromising as the man himself, she noted ruefully.

But she could feel glee welling up inside her just the same.

As simple as that, she thought in self-congratulation. She said to the reception clerk, 'Would you send the maître d'hotel to my suite right away, please. I wish to entertain a guest privately there to dinner tonight.'

The clerk stared at her. 'But our dining-room is excellent, *señorita,* and tonight there will be a musical show with folk dancing which you and your guest will enjoy.'

'I'm afraid not,' said Leigh in a tone which brooked no argument. 'My—guest and I have business to discuss which requires peace and privacy, so please do as I have asked.'

As she rode up in the lift, she re-read his note. So his time in Lima was limited. Did that mean he was going back to Atayahuanco very soon? It seemed more than likely.

But what he didn't realise, she told herself pleasurably, her nails curling into the palms of her hands, was that she would be going with him.

She devoted the rest of the afternoon to relaxing and getting ready, smoothing away any ragged edges with a leisurely session with the hairdresser and manicurist in the hotel's beauty salon.

Dressing that evening, she subjected her wardrobe to minute scrutiny before deciding what to wear. She felt rather like a general planning some spring offensive. And it was, she thought, definitely time for the big guns!

Her silky black dress relied for its effect on the chic and daring of its cut. It moulded itself lovingly to her slim figure before breaking out into a brief swirl of a skirt, and the halternecked bodice, although reasonably demure at the front, plunged well below her waist at the back.

She fixed delicate gold spirals in her ears, and added a discreet misting of Hermès, before deciding she would do.

Rourke Martinez, she thought smiling, would not know what had hit him.

The telephone rang promptly at eight.

'Your guest is here, *señorita,*' an expressionless voice told her.

'I'll come down,' said Leigh. 'Ask him to wait for me in the bar, *por favor.*'

She took a deep breath, as she gave herself a final considering survey in the long mirror. Black shoes with slender, spiked heels and pale stockings with embroidered seams completed her ensemble, and her hair gleamed like silk.

She thought, I look like a woman going to meet her lover, and the realisation stopped her in her tracks. For the first time, she felt a qualm about her plans for the evening, then she squared her slender shoulders, lifting her chin defiantly. However loathsome she might find it having to play up to a man like Rourke Martinez, it would be worth it, if it meant she found Evan at last.

And after the way Rourke Martinez had treated her, it would be amusing to see if she could make him grovel, even for a short while.

She caused a minor sensation as she entered the bar, but she would have enjoyed it more if she hadn't been working so hard to conceal her own nervousness.

She saw him at once, of course. He was head and shoulders taller than anyone else around, standing at the bar, with his back to her. Then as if alerted by the sudden hush which had descended at her entrance, he wheeled slowly, glass in hand, and looked at her.

He looked—arrested anyway, Leigh thought as she pinned on a cordial smile, and crossed the space which separated them.

'Doctor Martinez.' Her voice was warm to match her smile. 'I hope I haven't kept you waiting.'

'If you did,' he said slowly, 'you are undeniably worth waiting for, Miss Frazier. Is this solely in my honour, or are you expecting other company?'

'But I don't know anyone else in Lima.' Leigh lowered darkened lashes demurely.

'Of course,' he drawled. 'I was forgetting. May I get you a drink?'

She shrugged. 'Whatever you're having will be fine.'

His brows rose faintly. 'I'm having a pisco sour, but I should warn you, they can be potent.'

'When in Rome,' Leigh said lightly. 'Shall we sit down?'

It was working, she thought, as she reached into her bag for a tissue she didn't need. The stark uncovered blackness of the dress against her pale skin was a surefire winner. He could hardly take his eyes off her. Obviously women in model gowns were in short supply in the wilds of Atayahuanco. Well, let him eat his heart out.

Although she had to admit, as he brought the drinks to their table, that he didn't look like a man who would ever go short of female company, except through his own choice.

He was more formally dressed this evening, in a pale, lightweight suit with a dark blue silk shirt. And if she was the cynosure of all the masculine eyes in the bar, she could not deny that he was being surveyed with discreet avidity by the women.

Not that she could altogether blame them, she thought unwillingly. However much she might dislike him, she had to acknowledge that he was an attractive devil, and magnetically virile as well. And not lacking in charm either, she supposed, when he chose to exert it.

Smilingly, she lifted her glass to him. 'To our better understanding, Doctor Martinez.'

His expression was enigmatic as he returned the toast. '*Salud,* Miss Frazier.'

Leigh tasted her drink with a certain amount of caution. There was a tang of lemon, she recognised, and underneath it all, a kick like a mule. One, she thought, would undoubtedly be enough.

'So—how are you enjoying Lima?' he asked.

Polite conversation, it seemed, was the order of the day, and Leigh obediently picked up her cue.

'Interesting, but it has its drawbacks,' she said lightly. 'This constant mist, for one thing.'

'Ah, the *garua*.' He grinned slightly. 'Legend has it that when the Spaniards asked the conquered Incas where was the best place to build their city, the Incas recommended Lima with deliberate malice.'

She laughed. 'It wouldn't surprise me. But, after all, it wasn't Lima I came to see.'

'I suppose not,' he said smoothly, but across the table, the topaz eyes met hers in a clash like the ring of swords between two duellists. Leigh had to smother a slight gasp, but she forced herself to go on smiling.

'I feel I haven't had a chance to see the real Peru,' she went on.

'Lima is real enough,' he said. 'You'd be well advised to use your return ticket, Miss Frazier. Juanita at Peruvian Quest will help if there's any problem over the flight.'

Leigh sipped her drink, smiling coolly. 'Oh, I'm not ready to cut short my trip yet awhile. This dreadful mist can't last for ever, and I haven't seen Cuzco yet—or Machu Picchu. I hear that's really spectacular.'

He finished his drink, and set down the glass. 'Well, as long as you stick to the recognised tourist trails with an organised party, you won't come to too much harm. Now, would you like another drink, or shall we have dinner? There's a good place on the Carretera Central I thought I'd show you.'

Leigh put down her own empty glass. 'It sounds fascinating, but I've already arranged dinner, here in my suite.' She watched him digest this, then added sweetly, 'After all, I invited you—remember?'

His eyes swept over her in a lingering, frankly disturbing appraisal. 'I'm not likely to forget,' he said. 'And I'm still wondering why.'

'To make amends—build bridges,' Leigh said calmly. She gave him a brilliant smile. 'After all, there's no need for us to be bad friends, Doctor Martinez. We're on the same side.'

'Are we, Miss Frazier?' he asked softly. 'I think I might need some convincing of that.'

'Well, the night is young.' Leigh rose to her feet. 'So—shall we go up and eat?'

Her face was serene as she led the way to the lift, but at the same time she was aware of a distinct *frisson* of uneasiness. Rourke Martinez, she thought, was still proving a formidable opponent, although she thought she might be ahead on points—just.

She shook herself. She couldn't start losing her nerve now. He was a man, and capable of being manipulated like any other. And she had been adept at that kind of manipulation since her cradle.

There was no reason, no reason at all to think that this time she might have met her match.

CHAPTER THREE

THE dinner, at least, was everything Leigh could have asked for. She had ordered one of the house specialities, chicken cooked with peppers and hot spices. Rourke Martinez ate with unconcealed appreciation, but Leigh was too much on edge to do more than toy gracefully with whatever was set in front of her. She let her companion make the conversational running too, while she tried to marshal her thoughts, and decide on the best line of attack.

She had to concede that he was interesting to listen to. He touched lightly on such diverse topics as the ancient Inca civilisation, down to the current political situation. And he seemed, she realised, to be on nodding terms, or better, with any number of highly placed people in the government and the arts, although there was no element of name-dropping in what he told her. She was getting a glimpse of a very different world from her own, and under any other circumstances she would have revelled in it. As it was. . .

She studied him covertly under her lashes, wondering about him. The ambiguity of his name puzzled her, for one thing, but she was also intrigued in other ways, in spite of herself. She found herself wondering if he was married, and if so where his wife was. If he was single, he didn't look like a man who would readily accept a celibate existence. There was a definite element of sensuality in the curved lower lip of his forceful mouth.

He was peeling some fruit, and as Leigh watched the deft movements of his lean, long-fingered hands, an inexplicable shiver ran through her. She was almost glad when the waiter who had been serving them returned to clear the table and bring coffee.

She wondered if Rourke Martinez had been watching her watching him, and hurried into speech. 'Were you born in Peru, Doctor Martinez?'

He shook his head. 'I was born in your own country, while my father was in political exile there. And I was named for my mother's family. She happens to be Irish,' he added. 'Both my parents now live in the States.' A note of amusement entered his voice. 'What else would you like to know?'

Any number of heated replies suggested themselves, but she quelled them, dismissing the hovering waiter before she poured the coffee. He, she recalled, took his black.

The smile she sent him when they were alone was charming, but slightly self-deprecating. 'I apologise for my curiosity, but I suppose it's only natural under the circumstances.'

'What circumstances are those?' he enquired, accepting his cup from her.

'Well——' She permitted herself a little wistful sigh. 'We have been rather thrown together, after all. And I am a long way from home—and in a very foreign country. And I do seem rather dependent on your goodwill.'

'Desperate straits indeed,' he commented coolly. 'Perhaps you should have enquired more closely into my background before inviting me up here.'

'Oh, I'm sure that's not necessary.' It was agony having to keep her tone sweet and reasonable when she felt like up-ending the coffee-pot over his head.

'I know you must think that I'm—an interloper, and a nuisance, but I had to come here. You must see that.'

'I can see that you are here, certainly.' He drank some coffee. 'The matter in dispute is how long you should remain.'

Bastard, she thought. She summoned a sad little smile. 'Perhaps you're right, however. Maybe I didn't think the thing through clearly enough before I started. But I tend to be a creature of impulse.'

'How fortunate for you,' he drawled. 'That's a luxury most of us can't afford.'

'I suppose not. But I've had time to consider now, and I can see that you have a point.' Leigh looked at him through her lashes. 'I—I'm trying to apologise, Doctor Martinez.' She set down her cup. 'Won't you meet me halfway?'

There was a startled expression in the topaz eyes as they narrowed, but all he said was, 'If that's what you want.'

It would do for starters, she thought, concealing her jubilation. Before he knew what was happening, he would be eating out of her hand.

She smiled at him. 'That's exactly what I want.' She paused. 'Now that we understand each other a little better, shall we be slightly less formal? My name is Leigh.'

'It was on the message that arrived at the camp,' he said rather drily.

She poured him some more coffee. 'Ah, yes, the camp. Won't you tell me all about Atayahuanco, and your work there? It obviously means a great deal to you.'

'It would take much longer than the time I have available to even begin to describe what we're trying to achieve there,' he said quietly. 'And yes, it does mean a great deal to me, which is why I don't readily accept passengers on the project. We haven't the time or the resources to cope. Everyone has to pull his weight.'

'I'm sure they do.' With you and your whip standing over them, she added silently. 'Are there no women on the project at all?'

'We have a female nurse, June Muirhead on the camp. And Consuelo Estebán is one of our pottery experts. Did your—fiancé never mention them?'

'No.' Leigh looked down at the table. 'He was more concerned, I think, with other elements.'

'I can guess.' His tone was dry. He ticked them off on his fingers. 'The atmosphere, the cold at night, the food, the insects, the sanitation. . . Need I go on?'

'No,' she admitted, sighing. 'But you mustn't blame him altogether. It was—wrong of my family to involve the project in our personal—differences. Please believe it wasn't my idea.'

'Nor Gilchrist's either, I should imagine.' His mouth twisted sardonically. 'Were we perhaps expected to make a man of him?'

She flushed. 'That's unfair! It isn't his fault if he wasn't much use on the project. He was out of his depth from the start.'

'In more ways than one.'

Now what did he mean by that? she wondered. But at least he wasn't sounding quite so unsympathetic and dismissive as he had the previous day, apart from that last crack about Evan.

And then she realised with utter dismay that he was looking at his watch.

'Well, thank you for a delightful interlude,' he said. 'It's good to be reminded of the pleasures of civilisation occasionally.'

'You can't be going already,' she protested. 'Why, it's still quite early!'

'So is the start I have to make tomorrow.'

My God, she thought, and I've been fawning round him, and feeding him. . .

She put a hand on his. 'Oh, Rourke, please don't go yet. I hate being on my own. I've felt so isolated, so lonely ever since I got here. You can't imagine what it's like.'

'It's a long way to come to discover you don't like travelling alone,' he said drily, but he made no further move to leave, to her relief.

'No one should have to be alone, when there's no need.' Her voice quivered. 'Oh, Rourke, can you guess what I've been through this past year, with nothing but letters for company? It's such a long time to be separated from someone you love.' She let her lip tremble slightly. 'But you wouldn't understand. You probably find it quite easy to be totally self-sufficient.'

'I wouldn't say that,' he said slowly, after a pause. 'I have the same needs as any other human being.'

'Then you must know how I feel tonight. I've been lonely long enough, and you're the only person who can help. I don't want to have to wait any longer. Don't close your mind to me again. I'm desperate. Say you'll do what I want—please. . .'

'It will be my pleasure.' He rose to his feet, and lifted the intervening table and its remaining contents out of the way as if it had been a featherweight. Then he reached down and took Leigh's hand, pulling her out of her chair. Off-balance, she half fell against him, seeing the dark face swim before her startled gaze, the topaz eyes alight with mockery, and something altogether less easy to define.

Then she was in his arms, swept quite literally off her feet, imprisoned against his body, and she was being carried—into the bedroom, her dazed brain realised.

'What the hell are you doing?' The words emerged in a hoarse croak of disbelief.

'Only what you ask.' He put her down on the bed, and came down beside her on the yielding surface, his hands pinning her effortlessly to the mattress. 'You're quite right, *querida*. Why should either of us have to spend the night alone?'

He bent his head, and she felt the shock of his mouth on hers, warm and explicitly demanding. Too demanding. No one had ever kissed her like that before. No one had ever dared. . .

His lips moved down to her throat, where the little pulse throbbed wildly.

She said breathlessly, 'Stop this! You must be insane. . .' Her voice tailed away in a gasp of shock, as she felt his hand move caressingly at the nape of her neck. Realising what he was doing, she tried to pull away. *'No!'*

But he had already accomplished his task. As she moved, the unfastened halter of her dress came totally loose, and the bodice slipped down, baring her to the waist before she could prevent it.

The topaz eyes burned on her. 'You're exquisite,' he muttered. His hand lifted, cupped one small round breast, his thumb brushing almost lazily across its rosy peak, sending a signal her inexperienced flesh responded to with frightening urgency.

Leigh screamed then, a small high, terrified sound. She flung herself away from him across the wide bed, rolling on to her stomach in a desperate attempt to conceal herself, dragging the bedcover round her body.

'You're mad!' she hurled at him, her voice cracking. 'Leave me alone—do you hear? Get out of here!'

'Playing hard to get, *querida*?' Shattered as she was, Leigh could hear the thinly veiled mockery in his voice. 'But there's no need, and certainly no time. I've already told you I have to be off early in the morning.'

He was making no attempt to touch her again. Slowly, Leigh sat up, still clutching the bedcover rigidly against her naked breasts. She looked at him, trying to steady her tumultuous breathing. He was lounging on the bed, very much at his ease. His face was straight, but she could hear the grin in his voice as he said, 'Don't be coy, my beautiful Leigh. I can't make love to you through a coverlet.'

She said on a snarl, 'You won't make love to me at all. How dare you lay a finger on me, you swine! Come anywhere near me again, and I'll have you arrested for rape!'

'I wonder how you'd get on,' Rourke said thoughtfully. 'You invite me up here, for an intimate dinner for two. You persuade me to stay longer than I intend. You tell me a sad story of how long it is since you had a man, and insist I am the only one who can solve your problem.' He shrugged. 'I wonder what the authorities would make of that.'

Leigh was almost crying with rage. 'I didn't mean that—you know I didn't! You've deliberately chosen to misinterpret my words. All I wanted was. . .'

'To go to Atayahuanco,' he finished for her. 'But I've already told you that's not possible, and there was no ambiguity in my words,' he ended grimly. 'No, Miss Frazier, you miscalculated badly if you thought a few smiles and soft words would change my mind about you. Everything tonight—the food, the wine, that dress—was intended to seduce me, isn't

that so? Well——' He stretched lithely. 'You succeeded beyond your wildest dreams. Isn't that good
to know?'

'It's totally nauseating.' Her heart was beating so
hard, it was almost painful. 'Now get out of here. I
never want to set eyes on you again.'

He sighed. 'You disappoint me, *querida*. I'd hoped
you might resort to some rather more potent form of
persuasion. You have the body for it. The sight of
you, the taste of you has given me an appetite for
more.'

She drew a sharp, swift breath. 'You—actually
think I'd sleep with you to get to Atayahuanco? You
really are crazy!'

He laughed. 'Your motives are your own business.
I would have only one—to enjoy every delectable
inch of you for a few hours.' He gave her a mocking
look. 'But I still wouldn't take you to Atayahuanco.'

'I'd die sooner than have you touch me again,' she
said icily.

He shrugged. 'There we must differ. Because I
think if I touched you—really touched you—you
might even start to live.' He swung himself off the
bed, straightening his tie almost casually, and stood
looking down on her. 'But we shall never know, it
seems. *Buenas noches,* Leigh.'

It was a long time before Leigh dared move—long
after the closing of the outer door of the suite had
signalled his departure.

She caught a glimpse of herself in the mirror as she
clambered stiffly off the bed—half-naked and dishevelled, she was a far cry from the elegant vision she
had taken such pride in only an hour or two before.
Her face crumpled like a child, and she had to seize
on her self-control as her sense of humiliation threatened to overwhelm her.

No one had ever dared treat her so shamefully before, she raged inwardly. And she couldn't even pretend, for her own comfort, that Rourke Martinez had been either drunk or carried away by passion when he had inflicted this degradation. No, he had known exactly what he was doing. He had deliberately allowed her to create the situation, then turned it against her.

She stripped off the black dress with loathing, and hurled it into a corner of the wardrobe. Well, she never wanted to see *that* again as long as she lived!

She took a lengthy shower, scouring her body to rid herself of any lingering remnant of his touch. But the scented gel with its alluring, evocative fragrance didn't really supply the desired effect.

What I really need is a bar of strong carbolic, she thought savagely.

Even when she eventually got into bed, she couldn't rest. She still seemed to feel the weight of Rourke's body beside her, over her, crushing her down, his hands reaching for her.

Eventually she sat up, switched on the lamp, and said flatly and aloud, 'This is ridiculous.'

She supposed she could always summon a maid and have the bed made up with fresh linen, but that might cause comment. So, if sleep was out of the question, she could consider the other options open to her. She dismissed the idea of switching tomorrow to another suite, or even another hotel. There was nothing for her in Lima anyway. She might as well move on. But where?

Going back to England, admitting defeat, was out of the question. Besides, Evan might be in danger, and she couldn't think about her own comfort and safety in such circumstances.

She had more than one score to settle with Rourke Martinez, she thought bitterly. Undoubtedly, it was his harshness and lack of understanding of Evan's problems which had driven him away like that.

But she had already, albeit reluctantly, abandoned the idea of trying to get him dismissed from the project because of the way he had treated her. She was uneasily aware that her own conduct had not been above reproach, and that her complaints against him might indeed sound rather thin—as he had implied, damn him. She could—oh God—just imagine her father's reaction to her story. . .

No, the best, most dignified thing was to pretend it had never happened—wipe it from her mind completely, although that wouldn't be so easy when she had to face him again eventually at Atay huanco. Although then she would have Evan beside her, she thought. Even if he had gone off on some crazy hunt for Inca gold, he surely intended to return.

Suddenly she felt cold. She lay back again, tucking the covers round her. If only Evan hadn't gone off like that, without a word. Why hadn't he mentioned what he intended in his last letter? If he had stayed at the camp for just a few days longer, he would have got her message. He would have been here with her in Lima, planning their wedding. He might even have been with her now, in this bed, holding her so that she would never be cold or frightened again.

Leigh shifted restlessly. Except that she had never really believed in pre-marital sex. If she wore white for her wedding, she wanted it to mean something, and Evan had acceded to her wishes, with wry resignation.

'You're a mass of contradictions, do you know that?' he had whispered to her, when she had withdrawn gently but firmly from a situation that seemed likely to carry them both away. 'You're always so confident, darling, so sure of your place in the world. But underneath it all, you're really old-fashioned, aren't you?'

At the time, she had been delighted with his understanding. It had emphasised, she thought, how right they were for each other. But now she wished she hadn't been so uptight in her attitude.

It should have been Evan's mouth scorching hers in fierce, sensual demand. It should have been Evan's hands caressing her naked breasts for the first time. It was Evan's lovemaking which should have drawn that unquenchable shiver of response from her and not Rourke Martinez' cynical advances.

Oh, Evan, she thought miserably. Where are you, now that I need you?

She turned over on to her stomach, pillowing her head on her folded arms. Well, let Doctor Rourke Martinez gloat over his sordid little victory. The campagn was not yet over, and somehow—somehow, she was going to Atayahuanco to find Evan.

She could expect no help from Peruvian Quest, she knew, either here or in Cuzco. But she wasn't short of cash, or initiative. She would take one of the organised tours up to Machu Picchu, then hire someone to take her the rest of the way. Jeep, she remembered the girl Juanita had said, and mule. She grimaced in the darkness. It sounded like hell, but if Rourke Martinez could manage it, she could too. And it would give her the utmost pleasure to see the look on his face when she made it into camp at Atayahuanco.

On that thought, and against all the odds, she fell asleep, smiling.

The mule's name was Rosita, and she was said to be a family pet, but Leigh didn't believe a word of it. She was a scrawny animal, with a drooping ear, and a malignant expression in her eyes, and if she had had a choice, Leigh would have wanted no part of her. Only choices, she had discovered over the past few days, were pretty thin on the ground.

The first buoyancy which had started her off on her journey had begun to evaporate rapidly under the sheer pressure of the difficulties she had encountered

There had been no problem in joining an organised tour. The hotel had been happy to arrange it for her, and equally pleased to retain her suite until she returned, because, as she had explained, her plans were fluid.

And although the trip to Cuzco and Machu Picchu had simply been a means to an end, she had to admit she wouldn't have missed if for the world.

Nothing she had read, no photographs had prepared her for the scale and majesty of the ruins under their twin sheltering peaks. She had spoken glibly to Rourke Martinez about 'the real Peru'. Now, she felt, she might have made a first faltering contact with its extraordinary and splendid past. And even the fact that sightseeing was strictly regimented hadn't spoiled it for her. She wished she had been just a tourist, like the others. Wished she could have lingered, spent a night or two in the locality, shopped for souvenirs in the narrow streets and markets of Cuzco. Instead, she had to shop urgently for the things she would need for her trip—warm, practical clothes, a small folding tent, a sleeping-bag and cooking implements.

But there had been setbacks from the beginning. Her first mistake had been to attempt to enlist the help of the tour guide, who had stared at her with open dismay and disapproval as Leigh outlined her plans, and then told her flatly that her schemes were madness. Leigh suspected his main objection would be in returning to Lima with one fewer member of his party than he set out with. Probably looks bad on the records, she thought drily.

But he had certainly done his best to dissuade her. And she was sure she had him to thank for a daunting visit she had received from two policemen.

At least, one of them had been a policemen, uniformed and authoritative. The other man, plump with a drooping moustache and sad, shrewd eyes, could have been anyone. No introductions had been made, and he had left most of the talking to his uniformed companion. But however politely couched, the message was a definite one. Leigh had no proper papers, no authorisation for such a trip. Without the proper authority, no pass could be issued. Without a pass, there could be no guarantee of safety. And even with a pass, a woman, young, beautiful, and alone. . . Hands were spread, looks were exchanged. Her possible fate was left to her imagination.

'But I shan't be alone,' Leigh had protested. 'I—I'm going to join my fiancé, Evan Gilchrist. He's based at Atayahuanco on the Peruvian Quest project.'

There had been a silence. Then the plump man had spoken for the first time. 'You are certain of this, *señorita?* So how is it the disappearance of this man Gilchrist has been reported to us by the project director, Doctor Martinez?'

So he had actually shown some concern at last, Leigh thought furiously. And at just the wrong moment.

She said smilingly, 'Oh, Evan will have turned up again by the time I get there. I'm sure he didn't realise the upset he would cause by going off like that. I think he has dreams of finding a cache of Inca gold.'

The plump man gave a dry, harsh laugh. 'Inca gold,' he repeated thoughtfully. 'That is—amusing.' He lifted a hand and gave minute attention to his fingernails. 'You have perhaps received some message from your man, *señorita*. Some rendezvous has been arranged?'

'Not exactly,' Leigh said carefully.

He gave her a long steady look. 'Be advised, *señorita*. Go back to Lima, or better still to your own country. It is not safe for you here.'

'Thank you for the warning.' Leigh met his glance, her chin tilted.

He said quite affably, 'It is not a warning, *señorita*. It is an order.'

They had left her gasping. The visit had unnerved her, and for a while she had been tempted to do as they said, and run for cover. Then she told herself she was being ridiculous. They had been exaggerating, trying to put the frighteners on her, trying to protect their tourist industry. If too many foreigners went missing, it was a reflection on them. But she could afford to hire herself some reliable protection.

However, their visit meant that she had to proceed with a certain amount of caution in her search for a suitable guide. The desk clerk at the hotel had put her in touch with a couple of suitable guides, but both of them had politely but firmly turned Leigh down when they discovered where she wished to go. They preferred, she realised resignedly, to stick to the more lucrative tourist haunts around Cuzco.

She was close to despair when the waiter who brought her breakfast asked, 'You wish to go up to Atayahuanco? My cousin has a mule to sell. And in his village, there are many who would guide you there.'

My saviour, Leigh thought joyously. She said, 'How do I get to this village? And what's your cousin's name?'

'You take the *collectivo, señorita*. And my cousin is Pablo Ortega. He is a good man, and will not cheat you,' he added piously.

Now, with hindsight, Leigh could see she had allowed her enthusiasm to out-run her common sense.

The journey in the *collectivo,* a kind of communal taxi whose condition made those in Lima seem positively luxurious, had been a nightmare from start to finish. The roads had been appalling, many of them little more than tracks traversing the sheer edge of some stomach-turning chasm, and she had been crammed in with vegetable crates, and two families, one of whom had a baby who wailed continuously. After the first few miles, Leigh had felt like joining it. She closed her eyes as they rounded the worst bends, but she had a terrible suspicion that the driver did exactly the same.

When the interminable jolting and lurching finally ground to a halt, and she realised they had arrived safely at their destination, her feelings were a mixture of mild surprise and profound relief.

The village turned out to be an unimpressive collection of shacks, huddled dejectedly round a small square, entirely dominated by a massively imposing church. Leigh would have quite liked to visit this church while she was awaiting the arrival of Pablo Ortega, on the grounds that anything would be better than standing around in the square being openly stared at by the village's entire population. But the building was locked and impregnable, and seemed to have been for some time, and she managed to deduce from one of the women that the priest no longer came.

Nor did there seem to be any kind of store that she could see, or anywhere to buy a cup of coffee. She was almost convinced that she had reached yet another dead end, and that there was no Pablo Ortega and certainly no mule, when she heard the padding of hooves, and the jingle of harness.

The first setback was Señor Ortega's firm refusal to allow her to hire Rosita. How could there be any such arrangement, he demanded righteously in atrocious English, when there was no guarantee he would ever get his property back at the end of the hiring period? Such things were with God. It would have to be a sale or nothing. After all, the *señorita* would have no problem selling a fine mule like Rosita at the end of her journey.

It took an hour for a bargain to be struck. Leigh wasn't sure what the correct asking price for a mule should be, but she gritted her teeth and bartered vigorously, and eventually with much shrugging and sighing on Señor Ortega's part, the deal was made, and Leigh was having her first lesson in bridling Rosita, and loading her correctly.

It was simpler than she had originally feared, Leigh thought with satisfaction as she sat beside her small fire, and watched Rosita hobbled and placidly grazing a few yards away, but it had been a blow to discover that the mule's tack was not included in the price agreed, and had to be bought separately.

But worst of all had been her discovery that neither Pablo Ortega nor any other member of the community was prepared to act as her guide to Atayahuanco. Leigh had argued and persuaded, and offered generous pay, but they were all adamant. But in the next village, they assured her, only a day's stroll away across the *puna,* there would be many willing to help the *señorita.*

The thought of spending the night in the wilderness with only a strange mule for company was totally unappealing, but she had no choice. It seemed important too to leave the impression that she was in charge, not worried about a thing, so she buried her qualms under a bright smile as she loaded her gear on to the clearly reluctant Rosita, and the whole village turned out again to watch her leave. By their looks and gestures, it was clear they thought she was mad.

And perhaps I am, she told herself ruefully.

She walked steadily, thanking her stars that the track was clearly marked and the going easier than she had anticipated, but when the sun began to sink behind the towering, snow-capped peaks, she was glad to halt. Her muscles were beginning to ache with coaxing the recalcitrant Rosita, and her elegant boots were pinching too.

She collected kindling, lit her fire, and heated coffee and tinned beans as she watched the sunset turn the high snows scarlet, crimson and violet before fading into opalescent pallor. She watched entranced, isolation and nervousness forgotten, wondering what dawn would be like, and as if to reassure her that she was not entirely alone after all, a great bird appeared high above her, like some dark spirit of the snows, its vast wings stark and black against the fading light.

The breath caught in Leigh's throat. A condor, she thought, between disbelief and jubilation. She was actually seeing a condor!

It was one of the things her fellow tourists in Cuzco had asked eagerly about, but the guide's response had been dampening. Sightings were rare, they had been

told, although the great vulture of the Andes was now
a protected species.

Leigh grabbed her field glasses from the small tent
she had struggled to erect, and focused them as the
hugh bird wheeled and swooped in a display for her
alone. When it eventually dwindled to a faraway
speck, she sat back with a sigh.

The wind had risen as the sun went down, and in
spite of her weatherproof clothes, she shivered as she
hurried through her remaining chores and crawled
into the tent. She was glad of the security of her
sleeping-bag, but at the same time sleep eluded her.
It was the first time, she realised, she had ever lain
down for the night without someone else within call,
or at least on the end of a telephone. She tried to think
of Evan, to reach through the darkness and the sighing wind for him with her spirit, telling herself that
he was alone too, and probably afraid. But there was
no answering comfort, no sense of oneness in the thin
air of the night.

She slept at last through sheer exhaustion, but
there were tears on her face before she closed her eyes,
and her dreams were confused and troublous, where
she ran in endless pursuit of Evan through a vast
maze of mountains, her lungs labouring for breath,
only to have her way blocked at every turn by a tall
man with skin like teak, and tiger's eyes, who told her,
'This is no place for you. Go back. . .' While above
her, the vast wings of the condor blotted out the sun
as it descended to seize her in cruel claws, and carry
her away.

CHAPTER FOUR

LEIGH awoke with a cry, and sat up, her heart thudding hollowly against her rib cage. She swallowed, trying to steady her breathing.

Oh, get a grip on yourself, she adjured herself impatiently. You're not a little girl any more to be upset by nightmares. Wait until you really have a problem before you start going to pieces.

She felt like the prophet of her own doom when she emerged from the tent and found that Rosita and the hobble had gone, and so, one frantic all-encompassing glance revealed, had the tack, all her spare gear and the provisions.

Leigh fell to her knees beside the grey embers of the little fire, wrapping her arms protectively around her body. All the time she had felt so alone, someone must have been tracking her, watching her, waiting for the right moment to rob her. Her head throbbed, and she felt sick at the very thought, although some stark logical corner of her mind told her that she had probably escaped lightly.

She could only be thankful that she had used her shoulder-bag as a makeshift pillow, so that she still had her passport and what remained of her money. But even when added to the tent, and the clothes she stood up in, it didn't amount to a great deal.

She tried to calm herself, to think, to make some kind of plan. Pablo Ortega had assured her the next village was within easy walking distance, but she suspected their definitions of 'easy' might differ. She couldn't manage to carry the tent and sleeping bag, so they would have to stay where they were until she could acquire another mule and return for them. She bit her lip. She had had enough trouble getting her hands on Rosita, and she couldn't keep passing over handfuls of *soles* as if there were no tomorrow. Any more losses on this scale, and she would soon be running out of money, and that was unthinkable.

Or she could go back, she thought, then tossed her head, flicking her tawny hair back from her face with fingers that shook a little. That was defeatist talk. Of course she would go on. Every mile she covered, after all, was taking her nearer to Atayahuanco.

She glanced round uneasily, wondering if she was still being observed—if the thieves were planning further pickings. She picked up her bag and put the strap over her head, slanting it across her body. Her secluded stopping-point no longer seemed so safe or peaceful, and she couldn't wait to get away.

The tent looked forlorn, and she hated abandoning her one form of shelter, almost glad when a bend in the track finally hid it from sight. She began to hurry until she was almost running, her senses on the alert for some sign that she was being followed. Although what she would do if that should prove the case, she hadn't the faintest idea. She kept stumbling, her boots slipping on the earth and loose stones, and she forced herself to slow a little, because the last thing she wanted on her plate at this juncture was a broken or even a sprained ankle.

After three hours, she was conscious of a feeling of desperation. She was hungry and thirsty, and her headache had returned full force. Oh, where the hell was this village? She needed some aspirin, a police station, and a meal, not necessarily in that order.

Her boots were hurting again, and she began to suspect she was developing a blister. When she saw the glint of a tin roof in the valley below, she cried out aloud in sheer relief, and hurried forward down a steep gravelly slope. It couldn't be the promised village, but at least it was a sign of human habitation. And even the humblest shack would be better than nothing, Leigh thought feverishly, as she stumbled the last few yards.

It was a comparatively large dwelling, built of adobe bricks, and surrounded by cultivated land. A few chickens pecked round the earth yard which fronted the building, and a turkey emerged from some scrub gobbling with hostile curiosity as Leigh passed, but she hardly noticed. Her gaze was riveted on the loaded mule which stood docilely before the entrance.

Rosita, Leigh thought dazedly. She had caught up with her. At that moment, a man, tall and broad-shouldered, came out of the house and walked to the mule, making some adjustment to its harness. She broke into a run, her lungs feeling as if they were bursting. Her voice sounded high and cracked, like a stranger's. *'Por favor. . .'*

The man turned with almost shocking abruptness, and as he faced her, Leigh knew that her nightmare had returned. The dark face beneath the concealing shadow of a broad-brimmed hat, the topaz eyes, narrowing in angry disbelief, belonged to Rourke Martinez.

She tried to check her crazy, headlong run, but the impetus carried her forward, almost into his arms. His hands gripped her shoulders, ready to tear at her like the claws of the giant condor which had preyed on her in her dream, she thought, her head spinning, her breath catching dizzily in her throat.

She gasped. 'It was you—you robbed me. . .'

Then his shadow blotted out the sun, and there was nothing but darkness.

There was darkness too when she eventually opened unwilling eyes. Her whole body felt hollow and bruised, her stomach was raw, and her head throbbed. She felt like death.

Perhaps she was dead, she thought wildly, and this hot, all-encompassing blackness was some shallow grave, scratched out in the dirt. She tried to scream but no sound came, gulped in a mouthful of stale air, and collapsed back on what she dimly realised was a bed—hard, lumpy, and musty-smelling, but supportive.

The next time she awoke, there was light—a lamp, with a wick burning steadily. Rourke Martinez walked into its glow, and said, 'How are you feeling?' His fingers encircled her wrist, seeking her pulse, and she tried to pull her hand away.

'Where am I? What am I doing here?'

'That was going to be my next question,' he said grimly.

Memory was flooding back, and Leigh sat bolt upright glaring at him. 'You took Rosita! You took my mule. You were following me and. . .'

He shook his head. 'I've taken nothing from you. I didn't even know you were in the vicinity until you came running in from nowhere, and passed out at my feet, babbling some nonsense.'

'It isn't nonsense!' Leigh's voice rose stormily. 'I bought a mule in a village yesterday. I tied her up properly last night, but this morning she'd gone, and so had all my gear.'

'You're out on your timing, *querida*. All these adventures happened nearly three days ago. You've been ill. You've had an attack of *soroche*—altitude sickness. Didn't they warn you in Cuzco to take things easy until you were thoroughly acclimatised?'

Leigh sank back again. 'Yes,' she admitted sullenly.

He held a tin cup towards her. 'Drink this.'

She sniffed the faintly herbal aroma with acute suspicion. 'What is it?'

'Coca leaf tea. A remedy of sorts for the *soroche*, although rest is the primary cure.' He paused. 'José and Maria have agreed to let you stay here until you're fully recovered, and then José will get you back to civilisation somehow. I presume you've sufficient cash to pay him for the inconvenience.'

Leigh sipped the tea with distaste, although it was not unpleasant apart from a slight bitterness. 'Coca leaf,' she said. 'Isn't that. . .?'

'Yes.' His mouth curled slightly. 'But if you're hoping to get high on it, forget it.'

'I wasn't,' she denied curtly. Her head was clearing slowly. 'I saw a mule outside. It's mine.'

He shook his head. 'No, it actually belongs to José and Maria, but I've hired it from them, in exchange for the use of my jeep. It's a permanent arrangement. You can compare brand marks if you don't believe me.'

'Brand marks?' she repeated doubtfully.

Rourke's brows lifted. 'It should be on your certificate of ownership. You do have one?'

There was a silence, then Leigh said defiantly, 'It was a perfectly legal sale. Now she's been stolen, and I want it reported to the authorities.'

'Without a certificate of sale, you haven't a prayer.' He frowned. 'How much did you pay for this animal?'

'Eighty-five thousand *soles*,' she said defiantly. 'She was a bargain.'

He laughed harshly. 'You were robbed long before your mule disappeared, *señorita*, and probably by the same person. A *gringa* with more money that sense must have seemed like manna from heaven. No doubt the mule would have been sold back to you further along the trail, if you hadn't wandered off it.'

She had suspected she might have been lost, but having Rourke Martinez confirm it somehow made it worse.

She said, 'This José—does he have another mule—one that I could hire?'

'No.' The monosyllable was harsh and uncompromising. 'You've taken all the risks you're taking, Miss Frazier. The only place you're going is back to Cuzco in the jeep. I thought your visit from Pedro Morales would have convinced you that you were biting off more than you could chew, but you're more stubborn than any bloody mule, aren't you, *querida*?'

'So you sicked those policemen on to me!' she exclaimed furiously. 'I might have known!'

He shook his head. 'You over-estimate my influence. But naturally they were concerned about any crazy schemes you might have in mind, and would have done their best to deter you.' He gave her a contemptuous look. 'But not even their best was good enough for you, naturally. You've been cheated, robbed and ill. You could have been raped and murdered, but you're still hell-bent on your own crazy way.'

'I'm looking for Evan.' Leigh's heart was pounding again painfully. 'I'm going to Atayahuanco to find him, and you won't stop me. I'll walk behind you every step of the way, if that's what it takes, but you're not dumping me here!'

His face was thunderous, his mouth thinning. 'Forget it, Miss Frazier. I have better things to do than escort some spoiled, moneyed brat across the Andes. Have some sense, for once in your life. Go back to Daddy where you belong. You don't need Evan Gilchrist. The world's full of equally worthless layabouts. You'll soon find consolation.'

Her face flamed. 'You unspeakable swine,' she said thickly. 'I love Evan, and I'm going to be with him. You may be a little tin god up at Atayahuanco, but you don't rule me!' She was struggling with the blanket which swaddled her. No wonder she had thought she was dead and buried. This thickness of fabric round her made her feel positively claustrophobic.

She struggled free, only to realise too late that someone had removed her top layers of clothing, and that she was next door to naked in flimsy bra and briefs. A fact that Rourke Martinez was openly and cynically appreciating.

It wasn't just her face now. She was burning all over, but she wasn't going to give him satisfaction by grabbing for the nearest covering like some outraged Puritan.

He said softly, 'Then perhaps this will give you pause for thought, Miss Frazier. Do you really want to trust yourself to the company of a man who's already shown you very clearly that he fancies you? The nights can be long on the *puna*.'

She looked back at him, her chin tilted inimically, armouring herself in hostility. 'Well, the attraction isn't mutual, Doctor Martinez—or are you threatening me with the rape you mentioned earlier?'

He smiled, his eyes travelling down her body, reminding her starkly that he had half-stripped her that night at her hotel, and she had been powerless to prevent him.

'Rape is for the inadequate, Miss Frazier, I don't place myself in that category.'

She shrugged. 'Then I have nothing to fear. And I would have thought a real man would have respected someone else's woman.'

His mouth twisted cynically. 'Under normal circumstances, I would. But the fact is, *querida*, I don't believe you're anyone's woman—at least, not yet,' he added casually.

'You're—crazy,' she said huskily. 'I—I belong to Evan in every way. Why do you think I'm so—desperate to be with him again?'

He said harshly, 'I can think of at least one very good reason—and it has nothing to do with sex.'

His sudden change of tack startled her, but to her relief she had at last spotted her clothes, folded neatly on a small wooden chest which appeared to be the room's only furniture apart from the bed. And she had realised why it was so dark too. There was no window. She grabbed her jeans, and stepped into them, dragging up the zip, then began to fight her way into her shirt.

She said sharply, 'Well, whatever my motives— and they're no concern of yours—I'm going to find Evan.'

'Everything that happens at Atayahuanco is my concern.' His voice bit at her. 'And I'm not having the project put at risk because of your boyfriend's criminal tendencies!'

Somehow Leigh maintained her composure, although inwardly she was reeling. Had Evan really found something valuable? she wondered. Could he possibly have stumbled across the Inca treasure they had joked about? Had he scaled the mountain of glass, and found the golden apple? Even if he had, that didn't make him a thief. She wasn't sure what the law was relating to such objects, but she would find out, and if his discovery had to be handed over to the authorities, then all well and good. There was no need for Rourke Martinez to be so—scathing.

She said quietly, 'You have no right to say that. When Evan comes back he'll have a satisfactory explanation for everything he's done. And I'm partly to blame, if he has broken any laws. Anything he's done, he's done for me.'

'To keep you in the manner to which you're accustomed?' The dark face sneered at her. 'I don't doubt that, Miss Frazier. It's a pity no one's ever made you count the cost of the luxurious life you take so much for granted. Maybe a trip to Atayahuanco might do you some good after all. It might shatter that gold-plated complacency of yours for ever.'

They said words couldn't hurt you, but that wasn't true. His contempt left her feeling mentally bruised. She had never met anyone in her life before who had such a lousy opinion of her, or who had expressed it so openly, she amended silently.

She said in a low voice, 'I don't care what you think as long as you take me there.'

For a long moment, the topaz eyes surveyed her abrasively, then he gave an abrupt nod. 'I'm leaving tomorrow. If you think you can take it, then tag along.'

Leigh moistened her lips with the tip of her tongue. 'I—I left my tent and sleeping-bag back at my campsite when I found the mule had gone. Could someone fetch them, please?'

'No, someone could not,' he said mockingly. 'Even if they were still there, which is doubtful in the extreme.' His smile widened unpleasantly. 'You'll have to share my tent, Miss Frazier—if necessary. Still sure you want to come along?'

'Of course.' Bravado sharpened her tone. 'Although if I have a choice of animal, I'd prefer to sleep with the mule.'

He gave her an enigmatic look as he turned to leave. 'I'll try and remember.'

When he had gone, Leigh re-fastened her shirt. She had been too upset, shaking too much to make a reasonable job of it the first time around.

So—she was going to Atayahuanco, but she was unable to raise any sense of jubilation. If she was honest, her stomach was already churning at the prospect. It couldn't be that far away, but she might have to spend one, or even two nights alone with him.

Leigh shuddered. Well, she would see him in hell before she shared a tent with him. The blankets on the bed looked handwoven. Maybe this Maria had some spare ones she could sell, and Leigh could make herself a cocoon of them. A couple of nights under the stars wouldn't hurt her, she assured herself. The air might even help to rid her of the last, lingering traces of nausea and dizziness.

Or she might get pneumonia, she thought, her mouth quirking wryly, as she sat down on the edge of the bed, aware that her legs were still shaking. But anything would be better than sleeping in any kind of proximity to a man like Rourke Martinez.

Unwillingly she found herself remembering a different bed in a very different room, the weight of his body against hers, the heat of his mouth, the stroke of his hand against her naked skin.

Impatiently, she shook herself. Was she crazy? Those were things she shouldn't want to—didn't want to recall. So why did these particular memories remain so vividly, degradingly potent?

She asked herself the question, but could find no answer.

José and Maria were younger than she had imagined, and rather shy, but they warmed visibly at Leigh's lavish praise for the baby son, who was obviously their pride and joy. Their house was basic in the extreme, and it was clear that they took no more than a subsistence living from their land, but baby Juan seemed well enough fed, and entirely contented.

Leigh managed to do a deal with Maria for some blankets. She let the girl think she wanted them as souvenirs, thankful that the language barrier prevented any detailed explanations. She meekly accepted another dose of coca leaf tea, and by evening felt well enough to sit down and eat a plentiful bowlful of the savoury brown stew which had been simmering for most of the day on Maria's wood stove. It had a flavour all its own, and she couldn't recognise many of the seasonings which had been used, but she was hungry after her prolonged rest, and ate every scrap put in front of her.

That night she was slightly dismayed to find that the bedroom was used communally by the entire household, including some of the chickens, but aware of Rourke's sardonic gaze, she made no comment, nor gave any hint that she found the situation unusual in any way.

In the morning, Maria beamingly served them with a fried egg apiece, as well as freshly made bread rolls and sweet milky coffee.

Leigh took her time over her breakfast, then rolled up her blankets into a neat bundle, and went out to where Rourke was re-loading the mule. Now that she took a good look, she could see it in no way resembled Rosita. It looked well nourished with a healthy coat, and infinitely more amiable than Rosita had ever done, and it made Leigh squirm to remember how much she had paid for her. A halting conversation with José the previous evening had revealed that in spite of the waiter's assurances, Pablo Ortega had not been an honest man, but had rooked her abominably. José, and Maria to whom Rourke had told the story in their own language, had both found it highly amusing, but although Leigh had gone along with the joke, she had been privately seething.

'Can the mule carry these?' She handed the bundle to him, and he nodded briefly, without commenting. On her way back into the house, she stopped to look at the row of hutches which stood against one outside wall, and admire the plump guinea pigs they contained. As well as the feathered livestock, José and Maria kept a couple of dogs as big as Alsatians, which were clearly watchdogs, so the presence of the guinea-pigs charmed her, and she lingered.

'Aren't they sweet?' she said as Rourke came to stand beside her. 'It's incredible that people as poor as José and Maria can afford to keep pets.'

'They can't,' he said drily. 'What do you think was in that stew you enjoyed so much last night?'

The world tilted suddenly, and she felt cold sweat break out on her forehead as her *soroche*-outraged stomach threatened once more to heave up its contents.

Rourke Martinez added with unholy joy, 'I'm sorry if it destroys any illusions.'

It was his tone which cured her. He was waiting, she realised, for her to throw up, or faint, or have hysterics. Well, he was going to be disappointed!

By sheer force of will, she dragged herself together. The world stopped spinning, and her stomach quietened a little. She even managed a smile. 'I had no illusions to begin with.'

She wondered if it was the dawning of a reluctant admiration she saw in his eyes before he turned away, but decided it couldn't have been. Not that she wanted his damned admiration anyway, she reminded herself hurriedly. And she might well end this trip a vegetarian.

They'd been walking about an hour when Leigh asked, 'How far is it to Atayahuanco?'

'Far enough.' His glance slanted mockingly at her. 'Want to quit already?'

'Of course not,' she disclaimed indignantly, but it wasn't altogether true. He set a good pace, and her feet were aching. Also it had been downhill all the way, into a deep valley, and the further they descended the warmer it was getting. What it would be like at noon, Leigh shuddered to think. She wanted to rest, but would have bitten out her tongue sooner than ask. She was sure the speed they were travelling at was deliberate, designed to wear her down—and out.

She tried to take her mind off her sore muscles and potential blisters by taking an intelligent interest in what she saw around her. The valley floor was cultivated extensively, with fields of maize interspersed with reluctant pasture land. Someone must work this land, yet she could see no sign of any settlements.

She would have liked to ask Rourke about it. There were a thousand questions bubbling in her mind

already, but it seemed safer to maintain the curt
silence he had initiated since they set out. The situation was fraught enough without her giving him the
impression she was trying to engage his interest, she
decided with an inward grimace. And she hadn't got
a straight answer anyway to the one question she had
posed.

When eventually he did call a halt, she had to
restrain herself from giving a faint cheer. They had
reached the valley floor by that time, and had followed the stream which meandered there back to the
point where it burst out of the rock in a narrow, icy
torrent.

Leigh sank down thankfully on to the grass, leaning back against a convenient boulder. She wanted
badly to rip off the offending boots and bathe her
throbbing feet in the stream, but she didn't dare. Her
shirt was sticking to her, and her smart jeans made
her feel as if she was encased in cardboard.

Her companion on the other hand looked cool and
relaxed, totally untroubled either by the climate or
the distance they had covered.

Leigh watched him through her lashes as he rummaged in a pack, and produced some of Maria's
bread cakes and a couple of tin mugs.

'Lunch,' he said, handing her a share of the bread,
and indicating the crystal gush of the water. 'I'm
sorry there's no caviare and champagne.' A pause.
'Or stew.'

Her stomach shuddered, but her face, she hoped,
gave no hint of it. She said, 'You really think I'm a
lightweight, don't you?'

'On the contrary, I hope you're not, because this
time I think you've bitten off more than you can
chew.'

He thought she was going to crack up, plead to be taken back to civilisation in the end, she thought.

She took a bite of bread. 'I'm tougher than I look.'

'You'll need to be,' he said shortly.

'Is that a threat, or simply a warning?'

'Read it how you like.'

The terseness in his voice needled her, but on the whole it was preferable to the thinly veiled sensuality with which he had treated her the previous day. Clearly that had been just another ploy to persuade her to abandon the trip, like that cynical pass he had made back in Lima, Leigh thought, almost grinding her teeth at the discomforting memory. Rourke Martinez didn't desire her, and never had. To him, she was nothing more than a—a pampered nuisance.

A perverse idea prodded at her consciousness—an urge to change his attitude—make him look at her in a different light. It would be interesting, to say the least, to see if she could make him regret the way he had treated her. Maybe even make him suffer a little.

He deserved to suffer, she thought broodingly, after all the rotten things he had done to prevent her going in search of Evan. In fact, he and her father made a fine pair.

She chewed vindictively at a crust. Had she been right about that? Had Justin Frazier's long arm reached out from England and touched her here? Had Rourke Martinez been ordered to see that she returned home, suitably penitent?

The more she thought about it, the more utterly likely it seemed.

She watched Rourke Martinez covertly, as he replaced the mugs in the pack and untied the mule, aware of an odd disappointment as her eyes lingered on the firm arrogant lines of his mouth and jaw. No

Inca lord after all, or tiger either. Just another of her father's puppets.

And what a fool she had been not to realise earlier that he wouldn't have dared behave to her as he had done without her father's sanction.

The urge to get back at him hardened into resolve within her.

Now I know the name of the game, she thought, I can change the rules a little. A small, vengeful smile curved her mouth.

'Ready?' His shadow fell across her.

She looked up at him, letting her smile widen into gaiety and deliberate charm.

'Ready for anything,' she assured him lightly. As she got to her feet, she stretched, sliding her hands over her slim hips and flanks as she did so.

She saw him register the movement, the thrust of her breasts under her shirt, then turn away abruptly, and she could have laughed out loud.

Now, my dear Doctor Martinez, she addressed him silently as they began to move up the valley. Let's see who'll have the more interesting trip!

CHAPTER FIVE

BY THE time they made camp that night, Leigh's smile was wearing a bit thin. She was exhausted, and her right foot was hurting badly enough to prompt her to limp when she knew Rourke wasn't glancing in her direction. She didn't want a campsite. She wanted a hot tub, and a proper bed with clean sheets to collapse into.

She had suggested tentatively at one point that she might ride the mule, but he had looked at her with icy derision.

'The mule carries our gear,' he had told her. 'You, lady, carry yourself.'

Oh, I have, Leigh thought wearily, sinking down on to a patch of scrubby grass. And now I want to put myself down.

'Resting comes later.' Oh God, what now? She rolled over and looked at him, as he stood unloading the mule. 'You look for kindling, while I pitch the tent.'

'In a moment.' Leigh flexed her toes painfully within the confining boot.

'Now,' he came back at her grimly, 'that is if you want a warm supper. You're not a luxury passenger on this trip, Miss Frazier, so you do your share of the chores.'

Leigh stuck her tongue out at him as he turned away. It was childish, but she didn't care. He had given her the hardest time of her life today, not just physically, but mentally too. She had been warm, charming and approachable, bubbling over with questions about the terrain they were crossing, but each and every one of her conversational gambits had been blocked. She felt strongly inclined to say 'To hell with it' and relapse into an identical silence, but she didn't want him to defeat her again. She had vowed to make him squirm, and she would do precisely that, even if her facial muscles were aching almost as much as the rest of her weary body with all this determined jollity.

She was relieved to find there was plenty of dry wood around, and made the fire economically and efficiently.

'There you are,' she said, as Rourke came over with the pack of food. 'I'm not as useless as I look.'

'No one could be,' he said with brutal frankness, and her hands curled into fists. Oh, taking him down a peg or two, or even three, was going to be more than a pleasure!

Supper was soup, coffee and potatoes baked in the fire, with the last of Maria's bread. Leigh wondered what they would do for food the following day, and guessed that Atayahuanco was probably nearer than Rourke wished her to know.

She stole a covert look at him under her lashes. His face was brooding as he stared into the flames. He was probably plotting his next move to be rid of her.

She said dreamily, 'It's a beautiful night. I can't believe how much warmer it is at this altitude.' She stretched sinuously, fully aware that he was looking in her direction, then slowly and deliberately undid another couple of buttons in her shirt. 'It's a pity we're not near water. I would have loved a swim.'

'I doubt it—unless your taste runs to leaping into snowdrifts.' His voice was curt, and he was frowning as he reached into a pocket and drew out a slim case, extracting a cheroot from it and lighting it.

Leigh hid a smile. Well, she had never seen him smoke before. A sign of tension, perhaps?

She sighed elaborately. 'Do you have to be such a realist?'

'I think one of us needs to be,' he said drily, drawing deeply on the cheroot. 'I don't know which I find harder to take—your view of Atayahuanco as some kind of romantic adventure, or your—er—fiancé's concept of it as an undeserved prison sentence.'

'And which is nearer the truth?'

'The truth probably occupies some kind of middle ground.' He gave her a long steady look. 'But if you want to preserve your illusions intact, it would be far better to go home.'

'Without Evan?' she asked sharply. 'I wouldn't dream of it.'

'Well, I hope your dream doesn't turn into a nightmare.'

The conversation, Leigh thought vexedly, hadn't gone at all as she intended.

She gentled her voice deliberately, inserting a husky note. 'Oh, I wish I could make you understand. Are you married, Doctor Martinez?'

'No.' The butt of the cheroot went whirling into the fire.

She moistened her lips with the tip of her tongue. 'But you must at least have been—in love at some time.'

He looked into the flames, the expression on his face enigmatic. 'Or what passes for it,' he agreed laconically.

I bet, she thought with sudden savagery, remembering again, in spite of herself, the cynical expertise of his caresses.

'Is that enough? Don't you ever find yourself wishing for more?'

'Wishing for what one can't have is a singularly fruitless occupation,' he said sardonically. 'Or haven't you noticed?'

She decided to ignore that last question. 'I wouldn't have thought there was much beyond your reach, Doctor Martinez. Or do you consider yourself married to your work?'

'Hardly, but it isn't a life for a woman to share.'

'The—right woman might think there were sufficient compensations.'

'I doubt it,' he said coolly. 'But I'm flattered that you take such a close interest in my personal affairs, even if it is an unnecessary one.'

'We've been thrown together.' Leigh looked at him through her lashes. 'I think under the circumstances, I can be forgiven a little—feminine curiosity about the man I'm alone with.'

'Then contain your curiosity, Miss Frazier. Believe me, it's much safer that way.'

'Is safety really all that counts?' The words, the tone in which they were uttered, the curve of her body as she leaned towards him were all deliberate provocation. And his own slight, unguarded movement showed quite plainly that despite his aloof front, he was far from immune.

'In this situation, I'd say so.' His voice was short, and Leigh had to control a satisfied smile.

She had succeeded in getting to him a little, and there was victory in that, even if she hadn't guaranteed him the sleepless night she had originally intended. But you couldn't have everything, she thought, stretching again, letting her hands slide over the rounded line of her hips.

'Well, it's been quite a day,' she said with a little sigh. 'Unless there's anything you want me to do, I think I'll turn in.'

'The tent's ready for you.' He tossed some more wood on the fire, not looking at her. 'And we have an early start in the morning.'

Leigh got gracefully to her feet, smothering a wince as she put weight on her blistered sole. 'Are you sure you have everything you need?' She lifted her hands and raked her tawny hair back from her face. He didn't reply, and after a pause, she went on, 'Then I wish you pleasant dreams—Rourke.'

She was at the tent, when his voice followed her tersely. 'And keep the flap fastened once you're in there, unless you want to be eaten alive by insects.'

As presumably he was going to be, on the hard ground by the fire, Leigh thought, as she obeyed his instructions.

The tent was not a great deal larger than the one she had left on the *puna*, and stiflingly hot. He had spread out a sleeping-bag, which was chivalrous of him, she supposed, but there was no way she was going to climb inside it. It was far too warm for that.

By the light of the small lamp fixed to the ridge pole, she removed her boots and examined her feet with a certain amount of concern. Both were blistered, but with luck they would stand up to another day's walk, or at least she hoped so. She had brought some antiseptic ointment and plasters with her, but they had been stolen with the rest of her supplies, and she wasn't going to ask Rourke Martinez for assistance, and give him another excuse for trying to leave her behind.

Her father's instructions must be weighing heavily on him at the moment, she thought, smiling, as she took off her shirt and wriggled out of the close-fitting jeans. She rolled her clothes into a bundle and tossed them to the back of the tent, before stretching out on top of the sleeping-bag. It wasn't luxury, but it was better than she could have hoped. In spite of her brave words the previous day, she hadn't relished the idea of such enforced proximity.

She sighed, consciously relaxing, grateful that no one was expecting her to walk anywhere else, and she could be still at last.

Her eyes were already closing, her mind drifting into the agreeable half-world which separates sleep from waking, when she was suddenly, startlingly aware of disturbance—upheaval.

She shot upright, nearly cracking her head on the ridge pole, gasping, 'What the hell. . .'

Rourke said, 'I see you've taken over. The sleeping-bag, however, is mine, and I'd like it back.'

Her mind reeled as she stared at him in disbelief. 'What do you mean?'

'I mean I need my sleep too.' He reached past her and dragged forward the roll of blankets she had got from Maria. 'Yours, I think. Or couldn't you even be bothered to look for them?'

Her throat felt tight. She croaked, 'But you—I thought you were going to sleep outside—by the fire. . .'

He gave a derisive laugh. 'Then think again. Now, move over.'

For a breathless moment she thought he was going to lay hands on her, and she wriggled away, panic lending her agility in the cramped surroundings, clutching the roll of blankets defensively against her.

Rourke was unbuttoning his shirt, she realised, dry-mouthed, stripping it off. 'You—you can't. . .'

'Why not?' The topaz eyes comprehensively surveyed her state of undress. 'You have.' He unbuckled his belt, and Leigh shrank back further, biting her lip savagely. 'But don't worry.' His voice reached her softly, goadingly. 'I'm not going any further—unless, of course, you insist. Now, are you going to sleep on those blankets, or continue to use them as a barricade?'

She realised with chagrin that she had actually closed her eyes. She opened them now to glare at him, trying to ignore the shock to her senses evoked by all that bare, tanned skin. The dark briefs which were his only covering made only the slightest concession to modesty, she realised, with a tingle of apprehension.

She said, 'I'll sleep on them, if I can have the tent to myself.'

'Not a chance.' He was propped up on one elbow, watching her. 'Only a moment ago you were asking if there was anything I needed. It could be I've thought of something.'

There was no need—no need at all to feel so bloody agitated, Leigh told herself. He was just trying to turn the tables on her again, that was all. And the fact that his eyes were all over her didn't matter in the slightest. Her underwear was cotton and perfectly decent, and he had seen her in it before, for heaven's sake. In fact, he had seen her in far less, but that was the last thing she needed to remember.

She tried to sound dignified but nonchalant. 'Don't you think this joke's gone far enough, Doctor Martinez?'

'A short while back, it was Rourke,' he said pleasantly. 'Or did you forget?'

'No,' she said huskily. 'I think it's you that's forgotten—just who I am, and who you are. Don't you feel you're rather exceeding your instructions?'

'I wasn't aware I'd received any,' he said. 'Unless that's how you regard the come-on you were giving me in the firelight just now.'

She gasped. 'I was doing nothing of the sort. . .'

'That's a lie, and we both know it,' he said unarguably. He held out a hand. 'Now stop being coy, *querida,* and put down those blankets, and come here to me. I want to remind myself how delicious you taste.'

Leigh was burning up with humiliation, her little victory reduced to ashes.

She steadied her voice with a tremendous effort. 'May we drop this pretence, please? My father may have told you to chase me out of Peru by any means you chose, but I hardly think he meant you to go to these lengths, Doctor Martinez. Now, if you'll take your sleeping-bag, and leave me in peace, I promise I won't tell him about this.' She paused, swallowing. 'I—I realise, of course, that I'm partly to blame—because I—teased you, and I'm sorry.'

'I'm sure you are,' he said mockingly. 'Didn't anyone ever warn you, *amada,* never to dangle a meal in front of a hungry man, especially when you've been to so much trouble to remind him that he has an appetite? Could that mean you're a little hungry yourself?'

'No, it doesn't mean anything,' she said, almost despairingly. 'Rourke—I don't know what my father's exact orders to you were, but I know he didn't intend this, so let's just get back to square one and. . .'

'And get one thing straight,' he interrupted, and there was a note in his voice which sent a shiver trembling across her heated skin. 'I don't take orders from your father, or anyone else for that matter. As it happens, I've never spoken to him in my life, and his possible reaction to the news that I've seduced you is not my pressing concern. Do you understand me?'

'Yes.' Leigh pressed her hands to her burning face.

'I'm glad. And you, *señorita,* also have something to be thankful for—that I'm actually too bushed to reach out and discover whether under all that gloss and artifice there's a real woman hiding somewhere. Now, I suggest you put out the lamp and let me get some sleep before I change my mind.'

Her hands shook as she unfastened the blankets hurriedly, and spread them in the small available space, before obeying his instruction about the lamp. Darkness gave an illusion of privacy, but it was only an illusion, she thought as she lay down, curling herself into a small defensive huddle as far from him as she could get.

'You're as tense as a coiled spring.' His voice reached her after a lengthy silence. 'Relax, in God's name!'

'I'm trying to,' she said huskily. 'I know this is all a joke to you, but. . .'

'I promise you I never felt less like laughter,' he interrupted with weary impatience. 'May I remind you that you invited yourself along on this trip? If the facilities don't appeal to you, you have only yourself to blame.'

There was a certain justice in that, Leigh acknowledged with a small sigh, as she tried to uncoil rigid muscles. Everything that had happened she had brought on herself, and her ordeal wasn't over yet either.

She would just have to lie there quietly, and endure somehow until he was asleep, which, if his even breathing was anything to go by, would not take long. She pressed clenched knuckles against her teeth, hating him. Apart from that brief revelation that he had seen through her little game entirely, he was being unbearably casual about this enforced intimacy. What a fool she had been to think she could ever get under his skin in any way, she thought wincing.

In spite of her discomfort, she managed eventually to doze, but her sleep was fitful and disturbed, aggravated by unnerving dreams. With a rumbling growl, the mountain was falling on her, crushing her, robbing her of breath, and she sat up with a whimpering cry, gulping at the stifling air in the tent, as the low sinister boom reached her ears again.

'What is it?' Rourke had woken instantly too.

'There's a noise.' Leigh was ashamed to hear her own panic-stricken croak.

'It's thunder,' he said, after a pause. 'And a long way off.'

She hated the sound of thunder in the night, and always had.

'Is—is there going to be a storm?'

'Perhaps.'

She ran her tongue round dry lips. 'I—I don't like them very much.'

There was a silence, then Rourke said drily, 'I imagine you've been sheltered from most of the storms in your life so far.'

'Oh, please.' She was rigid again, sweat pouring off her. 'I can't bear it!'

'You won't have to.' In the darkness his hand reached for hers, and held it. 'Is this any comfort?'

It was the most prosaic contact, yet somehow her arm—her whole body was tingling—electric with a strange, inexplicable excitement.

It was fear, she told herself. Fear, and weakness from her illness, and tension. That was the only explanation for this sudden tremulousness at the clasp of his fingers round her own. And that wasn't all. She knew a wild ridiculous urge to turn to him, to cancel the brief space which separated them, and curl into the circle of his arms.

It must be some lingering delusion left over from the *soroche,* she told herself numbly. That was all it could be. He despised her and she detested him, and that was what she had to remember instead of letting herself be thrown by the first act of kindness and consideration he had ever shown her.

She managed a small, choke l, 'Thank you,' and buried her face in the blankets. In the morning, she would probably die of shame when she remembered how her own ridiculous cowardice had lowered her defences against him. But now, in the hot and humid darkness, while the distant thunder muttered and threatened, it seemed right to let her hand cling to his. In fact, in some odd, drowsy way that simple gesture seemed to encompass all the security she had ever known. Which is madness, she told herself, and slept.

Leigh came awake slowly, aware of daylight, and at the same time, an odd feeling of restriction. She thought, Where am I? as she opened reluctant eyes—then stopped, her whole body stiffening in shock as her memory returned, and, with it, the unwelcome realisation that the chaste distance between Rourke and herself no longer existed. That at some time in the night one or the other of them had moved, so that now she was lying against him, tucked into the curve of his body, while his arm lay heavily and protectively across her breasts.

He was still asleep, his breath disturbingly warm on her neck, and as Leigh attempted to extricate herself quietly and discreetly from his embrace, his arm tightened, drawing her closer to him, while he murmured a drowsy protest against her skin.

It wasn't just shock that held her half paralysed this time, but indignation. He had spoken in Spanish, but one of the words had been unmistakable in any language. A woman's name. Isabella.

This time, Leigh had no compunction about disrupting his rest. She pushed vigorously at his encircling arm, trying to slide out beneath it, but it was as if she had been clamped into some kind of iron bar, and as she struggled he woke too, and lay watching her, a faint smile curving his mouth.

'Buenos días,' he said, after a pause. 'Did you sleep well?'

'I suppose I must have,' snapped Leigh. 'Will you let go of me, please?'

'In a minute.' He sounded amused. 'Why the hurry? You seemed happy enough to be in my arms last night, while I was keeping the storm at bay for you.'

She twisted round to glare at him. 'I'm quite aware you think you're God,' she said icily. 'But I doubt whether even you have any direct control over the weather. Now, let me up.'

'So we're back to the autocrat,' he said pensively. 'I think I preferred the clinging vine.'

'No doubt,' Leigh muttered sourly. She had stopped trying to wriggle free. It was totally useless, and just seemed to entertain him. She tried another tack. 'You said something last night about an early start.'

His grin widened. 'But I didn't specify for what,' he pointed out dulcetly. His free hand lifted and touched her face gently, his fingers brushing her cheekbones, her small straight nose, and her parted, startled lips. The topaz eyes looked deeply into hers. 'And when a woman's slept in my arms all night, I expect at least a kiss when morning comes.'

At least a kiss. She tried frantically to analyse the words, and found nothing to comfort her at all.

She tried to sound dignified and casual at the same time.

'Doctor Martinez, I'm really not interested in any more of these games. We have a journey to complete, and so. . .'

'Thanks for reminding me,' he intervened sardonically. 'So let's start adding up the cost of this little package tour of yours. How do you intend to pay for your share of the food and accommodation, not to mention my services as guide?'

'I have money,' she began, and he laughed.

'That's your answer to everything, isn't it, *querida*?' He shook his head. 'Perhaps I prefer to be paid in kind—with the pleasure of your company.'

There was a note in his voice that sent her heart fluttering in panic against her rib-cage, but she managed a little scornful laugh. 'Pleasure? That's the last word to use in such a context!'

'Don't denigrate yourself, *querida*—or your capacity for enjoyment.' His dark head bent, and for a startled moment she was aware of his mouth grazing the smooth curve of her bare shoulder.

Leigh tried to pull away. 'Don't!' Her voice sounded high and breathless, and she wrenched at her self-control. 'That—that isn't what I meant, and you know it. You—you seem to have forgotten I'm engaged to be married.'

'On the contrary,' he said silkily. 'But at the moment, I have more pressing matters on my mind.'

He turned her rigidly resistant body effortlessly, so that she was lying on her side, facing him. 'Like this.' His hand stroked down the sensitive curve of her spine, and Leigh gasped involuntarily, her body arching towards him. At the same moment, she felt him release the clip of her bra. With a little shocked cry, she tried to snatch at the slipping garment, but he was too quick for her, tossing the flimsy thing to some oblivion at the back of the tent. Then for a long moment, he looked at her. '*Dios,* Leigh,' he said huskily, 'I had almost forgotten how beautiful you are.' He pulled her against him, so that she could feel the slight roughness of his body hair grazing her nakedness. 'Now we're on equal terms,' he murmured, smiling into her eyes.

She tried to say, 'No,' but no sound came. All she could hear was the rasp of hurried breathing—hers, she wondered insanely, or his?

But Rourke wasn't in any hurry at all. His mouth found hers slowly, as if he had all the time in the world, and with a magical gentleness that left her devastated, the battle to resist him over almost before it begun. She found she wanted to respond, to re-create the warm, languorous movement of his lips as they caressed hers apart.

Now, they didn't seem to be breathing at all as his kiss deepened into subtle exploration, his tongue flickering against hers. Nothing, she thought with growing wonderment, nothing in her admittedly limited experience had prepared her for this slow, sweet sensuality.

After a long time Rourke lifted his head and looked down at her. She stared back, lips parted, eyes dilated, unable to speak or even think coherently.

His hands lifted and cupped her breasts, already aching deliciously from the pressure of the hard wall

of his chest, and her stomach lurched dizzily in
excitement. A deep throb of need was beginning to
evince itself deep within her, and as his fingertips delicately brushed her erect, rosy nipples, a small greedy
moan was torn from her throat.

The sound of it shocked her back to a kind of sanity.

'Oh, God—stop. . .' Her throat muscles felt taut,
and her whole body seemed to be on fire. Desperately, she twisted free, rolling away from him in the
cramped space. 'You—mustn't!'

'Why not?' He was still close. Those strange brilliant eyes of his—tiger's eyes—were looking into her
own, as if in some way he was seeking her soul.

'For all kinds of reasons.' Leigh was babbling, and
she knew it. Knew, too, that in spite of her protests,
she wanted him to go on touching her. She wanted
to clasp his head between her hands, her fingers tan-
gling in his hair, and bring his mouth down on hers
again. She wanted him to teach her everything there
was to know between a woman and her man.

Only he wasn't her man—that was what she had
to remember, if she was to retain even a shred of self-
respect. She was of no importance to him, as he had
made clear over and over again. She was just a convenient female body for his enjoyment, and the
sudden unexpected pain of that realisation tore at her
like claws.

'Tell me one.' He was smiling again, face and body
relaxed in the certainty that she was his for the taking.

She said in a voice she hardly recognised, 'Because
I'm not Isabella.'

She saw the smile wiped away, his face hardening
into a bronze mask. He looked her over, and the

bleak bitterness in his eyes seemed to flay the skin from her body. She snatched up her shirt, forcing her arms clumsily through the sleeves, her shaking fingers making a nonsense of the buttons.

She had to say something to fill the silence, the appalling gulf which now stretched between them. 'Besides, I love Evan. I'm going to belong to him and no one else.'

He said expressionlessly, 'And are you quite sure he feels the same?'

Leigh wasn't sure of anything any more, but the implied slur on Evan fuelled her anger.

She needed to be angry; it was a safer emotion than any of the others he had made her experience.

'You're despicable!' Her voice trembled. 'There's no dirty trick you won't descend to, is there, to make trouble between us.'

Rourke shook his head contemptuously. 'You're wrong. Gilchrist is already in all the trouble he can cope with in a lifetime.'

'Because he's stolen a mule?' she came back at him. 'Because—maybe—he's found some hidden treasure, and kept it? How does that measure on the moral scale, Doctor Martinez, with your behaviour? Or is attempting to rape another man's woman perfectly acceptable as far as you're concerned?'

'You're beginning to sound repetitive, *querida*,' he drawled. 'Why don't you exercise a little honesty yourself, and admit that you wanted what was happening between us as much as I did.'

'Because it's not true.' Leigh grabbed up her jeans, and began to wriggle desperately into them. 'And you're vile—vile to suggest. . .'

'The truth?' he interrupted brutally. 'Well, have it your own way, *querida*. I hope your talent for self-deception survives your reunion with Gilchrist—if that happy moment ever comes.' He paused. 'And now, if you want hot coffee, I suggest you get the fire going.' He reached for his own clothes.

Outside, the clear pale sunlight struck her like a blow. She crouched beside the fire, trying to coax life back into the embers with dry twigs, telling herself that it was the acrid scent of woodsmoke which was making her throat ache, and filling her eyes with tears.

It must be the aftermath of the *soroche* which was making her behave in a way so completely out of character, she thought miserably. Or perhaps it was loneliness for Evan which had betrayed her.

She looked at the tiny tongue of flame creeping round her twigs, and sighed. That was how it began, of course, and if you weren't careful it could turn into a conflagration that could destroy your whole life.

Shivering, she sat back on her heels. And found herself wondering, not for the first time, just who Isabella had been.

CHAPTER SIX

WINCING, Leigh lowered her throbbing foot into the water, and held it there. The river was icy, and if she managed to avoid blood poisoning from her blisters, she would probably die of frostbite.

She looked at the swollen, swirling waters with distaste. Last night's storm had had more than one effect, it seemed, but both of them equally dangerous. Judging by one of the few remarks Rourke had tossed her way on the journey, they were going to have to ford this flood somehow.

She bit her lip. Yesterday's aloofness, the hostility of their first meeting—anything would be better than the kind of loaded silence which existed between them now.

He had fairly forced the pace, too, she thought resentfully, making no allowance at all for her inexperience in this kind of terrain. It had, on top of her emotional turmoil, been sheer physical agony walking on her blistered sole, but she hadn't dared allow herself to limp in case Rourke thought she was looking for attention or sympathy. All she could do, she thought, was try to be as unobtrusive as possible for the remainder of the journey. And when at last they reached Atayahuanco, and other people, perhaps this terrible inner confusion would subside, and she would start to feel safe again.

With a grimace, she extracted her foot from the water and dried it gingerly on her handkerchief. She was so engrossed in what she was doing that the first intimation she had of his approach was when his shadow fell across her, and she looked up with a little cry. 'Oh, you startled me!'

He disregarded that and squatted beside her, his brows drawn together in a thunderous frown. 'Would you like to explain what the hell you're doing? Or what the hell you've already done,' he added grimly, his fingers closing round her bare ankle before she could prevent him. 'Let me see.'

For a long moment he was silent, then he said a number of words in Spanish which Leigh was glad she couldn't translate.

'Are you completely crazy?' he bit at her. 'Why didn't you tell me you were in this kind of trouble?'

Because this is nothing, she thought, compared with the pain I feel inside.

She said quietly, 'I didn't want to bother you.'

'You'd rather risk your life?' he demanded derisively, and saw her flinch. 'Don't you realise you can't fool with your health in this wilderness? There's no convenient casualty department to take you to out here.'

Leigh reached for her sock, letting her hair swing forward to conceal her face. 'I'm sorry,' she said in a constricted voice.

'And don't put that on,' he ordered impatiently. 'I've some dressings in one of the packs, and an ointment the Quechua seem to use for everything from snakebite down. We'll see what that does, and tonight you'll get some proper medical attention.'

'At Atayahuanco?' In the flood of relief at the thought, there was a treacherous pang of a very different emotion, and she looked down, swiftly veiling her eyes with her lashes in case she gave anything away.

'No—that's still a day and a half's march away. A friend of mine runs a clinic of sorts from one of the villages. We'll have to gamble on him being there, and not off on one of his vaccination programmes.'

'I didn't mean to be such a nuisance.' Still, she didn't look at him, as awkwardly she tried to struggle to her feet.

'And don't put that foot to the floor,' Rourke said sharply.

Leigh stood one-legged like a stork, clutching her boot and sock. 'If you could find a stick. . .'

He said something under his breath, and sliding an arm under her knees, swung her up into his arms like a child, holding her as closely, she thought, her heart racing, as he had that night in Lima when he had carried her into the bedroom. And that, dear God, was the last thing she needed to remember. . .

The ointment was a greyish colour, and smelled foul, but it felt soothing, she had to admit, as Rourke applied the dressing to her foot. She looked at the dark down-bent head, longing to press her lips to his dishevelled hair, and wished there were an old Indian palliative for frustration too. Because that was what it all about—the inner trembling, the hunger to touch and be touched. She needed to see Evan again, she told herself. When she had the security of his love wrapped round her once again, this anguish of emotional confusion would vanish like morning mist. It would have to, she thought, digging her nails into the palms of her hands.

Rourke noticed, of course. 'Am I hurting you?'

Terminally, she thought. Aloud, she said, 'No—I'm just not very brave.

He gave her a dry look. 'If you say so.' He got to his feet. 'That will have to do for now. Tonight I'll get Greg to give you a shot of something. We don't want to take any chances.'

No, thought Leigh, as she manoeuvred her sock over the dressing, we don't. She wondered if the unknown Greg could administer some kind of general anaesthetic to numb this strange inner pain she was experiencing—or even to stop her thinking altogether. She would be glad to be on the move again, and able to focus all her concentration on her physical discomforts.

Which were likely to be re-focused entirely, she realised as Rourke came over to her, leading the mule.

'Today you ride,' he said, making it clear it was more a command than a suggestion.

As she accustomed herself to the saddle, Leigh found herself thinking that this remote kindness was somehow worse than passion, or even the contempt he had shown her in their earliest encounters. The conflict between them in the past had been disturbing, even infuriating, but it had made her feel alive. Now, there was this barrier of silence and reserve between them, and it was all of her own making, she supposed wretchedly, although she couldn't have allowed him to go on making love to her as he had been doing. She had had to stop him somehow.

He must have loved this Isabella very much to have reacted as he had done to the mention of her name.

Perhaps he loves her still, she thought, sinking her teeth into the soft inner fullness of her lip, as pain lanced through her again.

She was being ridiculous, and she knew it. In spite of everything that had happened between them, Rourke Martinez was still virtually a stranger to her. If she counted up on her fingers the hours she had spent in his company, he would barely be an acquaintance, she supposed—and she was engaged to another man, and yet her own reaction to the idea of this other woman in his life was something akin to jealousy.

No, she thought desperately, it can't be that. It can't be. There's no reason. . .

She was ashamed of how she felt. Ashamed of how she had responded to his mouth, and the touch of his hands on her body. Ashamed of the means she had used to escape him, which had driven him into this tight-lipped introspection.

And in the mean time, she thought, there was the more practical problem of how they were going to get across this river. Rourke left her with the mule while he went scouting ahead downstream. When he returned, he was frowning.

'There is a spot,' he said curtly. 'But it won't be easy.'

Leigh swallowed. 'I'm sorry.'

His brows flicked upwards in surpise. 'Why should you be? You were hardly responsible for conjuring up last night's storm—or its aftermath,' he added, sending her an enigmatic glance.

She felt involuntary colour warming her face. 'I— I meant I was sorry for inflicting myself on you—giving you extra responsibility. You'd be getting on much faster without me.'

He shrugged. His voice abrupt, he said, 'It's too late to concern ourselves with that now.'

When they reached the place he had found for them to cross, Leigh thought with dismay that he hadn't exaggerated. It was slightly narrower at this point, it was true, but the water looked deep, and fierce and unwelcoming.

'Wait here,' Rourke directed briefly. 'I'll take the mule across, and come back for you.'

Leigh sat down on a fallen tree trunk and watched as he cut himself a stick from a convenient branch, the colour rising helplessly in her cheeks as he stripped down to his briefs, wedging his clothes into one of the mule's packs.

The animal was reluctant at first, but he coaxed her down the bank, and into the water, testing the riverbed with his stick before taking each step.

Leigh was relieved to see that the water seemed to be hardly more than waist-deep. After a slight hesitation, she followed Rourke's example and took off her outer clothes, and footwear, rolling them into a bundle to carry across.

Rourke, she saw, had nearly reached the other side, still treading cautiously, and she decided to follow, rather than put him to the inconvenience of fetching her.

The chill of the water took her breath away for a moment, and she paused, gasping, aware at the same time of the deep drag of the current. She hadn't bargained for that, she thought ruefully, or for the fact that the riverbed was littered with round loose stones which made every step a hazard. And Rourke had made it look so easy!

She heard him shout angrily, telling her to go back, but she pretended she hadn't heard above the noise of the water, and soldiered on. The water was nearly up to her chest now, and keeping her bundle of clothing dry was beginning to make her arms ache, although she had reached less than halfway. The current seemed stronger here too, pulling at her with real force, so that every step was a battle.

She moved, realised she was slightly off balance, and tried to recover herself, felt her foot slip on a stone, and fell sideways, crying out in terror as the dark waters closed over her.

Choking and gasping, she fought her way to the surface, trying to regain her footing, but it was impossible. The current had her, like a leaf caught in a millrace, and was sweeping her away. She struck out wildly. She had always thought of herself as a good swimmer, but these waters were too strong and angry for her, and she submerged again. Somehow she struggled back to the surface, eyes streaming, lungs bursting, half deafened.

A man's voice, hoarse and unrecognisable, was shouting, 'The tree—grab the tree!'

Dimly, Leigh was aware of a tangle of branches ahead of her, above her, and she reached up with a desperate strength she hadn't known she possessed, and caught at them with a force which threatened to wrench her arm out of its socket. Crying out with pain, she hung there one-handed, feeling the water tear at her, trying to drag her away.

She moaned, trying to draw air into her lungs, and heard Rourke's voice, impossibly near, say, 'I have you. Let go the tree!'

She obeyed, her bruised shoulder wincing at the movement. He held her against him, until she had regained her footing, then, very slowly, holding her clamped to his side, he began the journey to the other bank.

It seemed to take forever. Leigh kept her eyes tight shut, terrified that they would both be swept away, but somehow, agonisingly, they made it.

The roar of the water was muted now, she realised dazedly, and there was grass under her clutching hands. She collapsed, feeling weak tears squeeze out from under her eyelids, retching a little from the water she had swallowed. After a while the world stopped spinning sickeningly round her, and she sat up gingerly. Her body felt sore. There was a deep graze on

her leg, and numerous scratches and abrasions on her
arms and shoulders. She looked round for Rourke.

He was sitting a few feet away, his knees drawn up
to his chin, his forehead resting on his folded arms,
as he struggled to control his laboured breathing.

She thought, We could have been drowned—and
it's all my fault, and a little sob rose in her throat,
compounded partly of fear, partly remorse.

Rourke must have heard the little sound she made,
because his head came up sharply, and he stared at
her, almost as if he had never seen her before.

The sun was hot, but she was suddenly shivering
violently. She said in a small half-strangled whisper,
'I'm so sorry—oh God, I'm so sorry. . .'

He got to his feet, and stood over her, the topaz
eyes blazing.

'Sorry?' he repeated softly. 'Are you quite insane?
You disobey me—you risk your life—both our lives,
and you say you're sorry?'

'I know—I know.' The weak, shaming tears were
back, pouring down her face.

He said something under his breath, and came
down on one knee beside her. '*Dios,* Leigh, I should
not have spoken as I did. Don't cry, *querida.*' Gently
his fingers brushed her face. 'There's no need. By
some mercy, we are both safe.'

Her hand went up and clasped his, pulling it down
to her lips. He stiffened, trying to snatch it away, then
paused, his eyes almost torturedly searching her face.
His own hand reached out, reluctantly, to tangle in
her damp hair, and then they were kissing, their
mouths locked frantically together in a giving and a
taking sharpened by the danger they had been in as
well as desire.

Leigh was pliant in his arms, willing to follow
wherever he might lead. There was no mockery in

Rourke's kisses, no seductive beguilement, only a driving need which she recognised because she shared it.

She was aware in some strange way of every blade of grass touching her back, of every drop of moisture from her body mingling with his, as if until that moment she had only been half conscious of her physical being.

Now she was awake, and free, her hands restlessly shaping his broad shoulders, the long muscular curve of his naked back, her tongue moving against his with the same wild abandon. Her skin felt on fire, clamouring for his caresses, her breasts aching to be touched.

The heated pressure of his body against hers told her that he was deeply and passionately aroused, but in spite of her inexperience, she was neither afraid nor embarrassed. She wanted to know and be known totally—completely, she thought feverishly, as her hands slid down his body, seeking and welcoming.

For a moment he tensed at her first, shy overtures, then with a little groan of encouragement he lowered his mouth to her breasts, tugging the wetly clinging fabric of her bra aside with his teeth before encircling one taut pink nipple with his lips.

The pleasure of it was shocking, scorching along her veins. The sun dazzled against her languidly closed eyelids, and the delight he was teaching her dazzled her senses. Her breath escaped between her parted lips on a little sigh, as his hand stroked the curve of her hip, then moved downwards, slowly, searchingly, intimately. His fingers on her body were like the whisper of silk, but, at the same time, wickedly, devastatingly sure.

Every sense, every nerve she possessed seemed to be turning inwards, focusing on some sweet central core of physical hunger. It was difficult to breathe, to think of anything but this savage sweetness that his hands and mouth were creating. The current had her, she thought dizzily, was carrying her away for ever. . .

Then, as suddenly as it had begun, it was over. With a violent exclamation Rourke rolled away from her and lay prone, his head turned from her, pillowed on his folded arms.

For a moment Leigh lay still, her quivering body in turmoil, then slowly she lifted herself on one elbow and looked at him. She felt bewildered, totally bereft, unable to find an explanation for this uncompromising rejection.

He had once taunted her about her inexperience, she remembered painfully. Had he recalled this now, and drawn back because of it? Or had she, through ignorance, given him the impression that she was in some way unwilling? Didn't he realise—couldn't he tell how desperately she wanted him? And he wanted her—she was sure of it.

She put out a tentative hand and touched his bare shoulder. 'Rourke?'

He moved convulsively, shaking her hand away. 'What is it?'

'I don't understand.'

He sat up, pushing back his damp hair with a kind of weary impatience. 'What is there to understand?' he asked harshly. 'For a while we both went a little mad, that's all. Now it's over.'

'Just like that?' The enormity of it made her voice falter. How could he so easily dismiss that passionate, yearning intimacy they had shared, however briefly? His hunger had been as deep as hers, she would swear to it. 'Don't I have some say. . .?'

'There is nothing more to be said,' he interrupted flatly. 'You are, after all, engaged, and the last thing I need is this kind of involvement.' He got to his feet and went over to the mule, peacefully grazing a few yards away, to retrieve his clothing. 'Now, get dressed, and we'll be on our way.'

In spite of the heat, Leigh was shivering violently, her arms wrapped protectively round her body. Her voice sounded strange and husky in her ears as she said, 'I—I haven't got my clothes. I was carrying them when I slipped. I don't know what's happened to them.'

There was a long and terrible silence. Rourke lifted clenched fists and looked up at the sky. *'Madre de Dios!'* he spat. 'What else can happen?'

He drew a deep, furious breath, then began rummaging through the packs. One by one, a clean khaki shirt, a leather belt, and one of Maria's blankets landed beside Leigh on the grass. 'Have the goodness to manufacture yourself some kind of covering.' His tone was ominous.

The shirt was enough on its own, she thought, when she had scrambled into it. Cinched in at the waist by the belt, it still reached three-quarters of the way down her slender thighs. She carried the blanket back to him. 'I don't need this.'

He gave her a swift, comprehensive glance, his firm mouth thinning. 'That, *señorita*, is a matter of opinion.'

Leigh, as she turned away, began to wonder if she had dreamed those moments in his arms. Only minutes before, she had been on the brink of surrender as he had explored and caressed every secret of her womanhood. Now, it seemed, he couldn't even bear to look at her. The tears he had kissed away were threatening to overwhelm her again, but this time her pride would not let them fall.

She waited in silence while he made the mule ready, and still without speaking, accepted his assistance back into the saddle.

For a moment he stood looking up at her, the dark brows drawn arrogantly together. Then he said quietly, 'Danger makes us vulnerable, Leigh. We shall take no more risks.' He took the mule's bridle. '*Adelante.*'

The village was small, a narrow main street lined with single-storey adobe houses, opening out into a small square. Greg Mayhew's clinic, indistinguishable from any of the other buildings, lay at the end of an alley leading off the square.

In response to Rourke's jangle of a rusting iron bell hanging beside the front entrance, the door was flung open, and a broad, blond man with a beard stood staring at them. For a moment his eyes widened incredulously, then with a whoop of joy he dealt Rourke a blow on the shoulder which would have felled a lesser man.

'You old son of a gun! Where the hell did you spring from? And what. . .?' He took another look at Leigh, discreetly muffled, at the approach of sunset, in Maria's blanket. 'I mean—who is this?'

'This is Leigh Frazier,' Rourke said shortly. 'I'm escorting her to Atayahuanco. She has a blistered foot, and some other abrasions I'd like you to take a look at.'

'Anything you say.' Greg Mayhew moved forward and lifted Leigh down from the saddle. 'In you come, honey. You look really bushed!'

The small surgery didn't seem to have much in the way of equipment, but it was spotlessly clean. In response to Greg's shout, an Indian girl in a white overall came running, to help remove the shrouding blanket, her round placid face expressing open astonishment when she saw what Leigh was wearing beneath it.

She saw the same look, fleetingly, on Greg Mayhew's face before he turned away, busying himself with cottonwool and dressings.

She said, 'I nearly drowned today—entirely through my own fault. I was lucky to lose only my clothes.'

'Hm.' He took her pulse and blood pressure, and shone a light into her eyes.

As he examined her, he questioned her about the inoculations she had had back in England, particularly the date of her last anti-tetanus booster, appearing satisfied with what she told him.

He was a big man, but his hands were deft as he cleaned up her grazes and re-dressed her foot.

'I guess you'll live, Miss Frazier,' he commented laconically when he had finished. 'Especially with a square meal inside you. And my housekeeper Carlota has a daughter around your size, so we can fit you up with something to wear too.'

Leigh bit her lip. 'Doctor Mayhew, you must be wondering what I'm doing here. . .'

'It's none of my business,' he said amiably. 'And the name's Greg. The problem's going to be accommodation. The town's full tonight for the fiesta, and the only space I have left is the storeroom. It's not the kind of five-star Hilton treatment you're accustomed to.'

Leigh looked at him steadily. 'How do you know what I'm accustomed to?'

He shrugged. 'Your hands, your voice—all kinds of things, lady.' He shook his head. 'You survived your river ducking okay, but I'd say you were in culture shock.'

Leigh lifted her chin. 'Perhaps, but I'll survive that too.'

His mouth twisted slightly. 'Whatever you say,' he agreed. 'Now I'll go and see about some supper.'

'Guinea-pig stew?' Leigh began to re-button Rourke's shirt, wincing slightly. The stuff Greg had applied to her grazes had stung sharply.

He gave a shout of laughter. 'Oh, I think we can do better than that.' The glance he sent her as he left the room was slightly more approving than his previous expression had been.

But he was still wary of her, Leigh realised, and wondered why.

Carlota was a stout, stolid-looking woman, but her smile, although revealing broken and discoloured teeth, was as warm as the sun. Over her arm she was carrying a woven skirt, thick with embroidery, and a blouse of unbleached cotton with full sleeves and a drawstring neckline. Her English was limited, but Leigh soon grasped that these garments were the pick of the unknown daughter's wardrobe, and expressed herself with suitable delight and gratitude, to Carlota's obvious gratification.

To Leigh's surprise, she found herself conducted to the rear of the house, and a large verandah already crowded with people, sitting in groups drinking *chicha* and smoking, while children played between them. Carlota led Leigh firmly to the end of the verandah, to a ramshackle erection of wooden screens, and urged her into their shelter. Inside, incredulously, Leigh found a bowl of gently steaming water, a cake of fresh soap, and a towel.

'You wash,' Carlota explained laboriously, with a vigorous mime. 'I rinse.'

At any other time, Leigh might have demurred at the dubious privacy of the arrangements, but the thought of being able to take what amounted to her first warm shower since the hotel in Cuzco outweighed every other consideration. Luxuriously she lathered her body, then, as an afterthought, applied some soap to her hair, digging her fingers into her scalp. It was a far cry from the expensive shampoo she normally used, which had vanished with the rest of her gear, but it felt heavenly. And when she was ready, Carlota, puffing a little, mounted a stool outside the little cubicle, and poured a steady torrent of tepid water all over her from a bucket.

When she had towelled off, Carlota's arm appeared holding the blouse and skirt, to which had been added a pair of frilly nylon panties, which spoke far more of Lima then this village. Leigh dressed swiftly, adjusting the neckline of the blouse to a reasonably modest level, wishing, as she did so, that the soft fabric didn't cling to the untrammelled outline of her breasts quite so revealingly.

She felt absurdly self-conscious as Carlota led her back along to the verandah to the house. There was an enticingly savoury smell in the air, and Leigh found her mouth watering involuntarily, as Carlota smilingly indicated a door to her, and vanished. She moved forward slowly. The soft leather slippers which Carlota had also supplied were rather too large, and made no sound on the beaten earth floor.

As she bent to adjust one of them, through the half-open door she heard Greg Mayhew's voice, clear and faintly irascible. 'Are you out of your head, man? What the hell are you doing with this *chica?* Didn't you learn your lesson from Isabella?'

For a moment Leigh stood motionless, her heart thudding. Then, still in silence, she fled back the way she had come.

CHAPTER SEVEN

LEIGH was sitting cross-legged on the verandah, looking down at the swaddled baby she had been given to hold, when a footstep sounded beside her, and Rourke was looking down at her.

His face was enigmatic, the topaz eyes hooded as he said, 'Supper's ready. Did Carlota forget to mention it?'

'I must have misunderstood.' She handed the baby back to his mother, and stood up, brushing down her skirt, hoping that the dim light from the verandah's smoky lamps would disguise the rising colour in her face. 'I'm starving as well.' She was aware she was babbling, trying to cover the rawness of heart and mind which was assailing her.

But she wasn't confused any more. She had come halfway across the world to find the love of her life, and contrary to all her beliefs and expectations, she knew now that he was standing in front of her, and the pain was almost more than she could bear.

She knew that what she had felt for Evan was simply a passing fancy, given extra importance by their enforced separation. Her father had been wrong for once, she thought wryly. If he had forced them together, instead of apart, she would probably have realised her mistake much sooner.

As it was, it had taken humiliation, hardship and danger to reveal to her what it was she wanted most in the world—and it was beyond her reach. She, who had never been denied anything in her short life! The irony of it was almost murderous.

Eyes downcast, she allowed Rourke to escort her back to the living-room. It was primitive enough, she saw in the lamplight. There was a stove for heating, a hard-looking couch covered in blankets, and a rickety table with some folding chairs.

Greg Mayhew's smile was welcoming, but there was a reserve in him as he courteously seated her at the table. There was a thick bean and potato soup, followed by a rice dish, savoury with onions, tomatoes and herbs and accompanied by mutton stew. In spite of her unhappiness, Leigh found she was ravenous, and ate every mouthful placed in front of her. The men drank *chicha,* but Leigh was offered and accepted cola.

The conversation was general, and Leigh was brought into it in a way which excluded her as completely as if they had ignored her. They were being civil to the outsider, that was all, she thought ruefully.

'So what brings you to this part of the world, Leigh?' Greg asked at last, as they sat drinking mugs of milky rather sweet coffee.

Leigh moved a shoulder. 'I came to find someone,' she said evasively. She thought, I came to find myself first, although I didn't know it. Then I found Rourke. She had to resist the impulse to look at him in case her eyes betrayed her.

'She came to find her fiancé.' There was an undisguisedly harsh note in Rourke's voice. 'A man called Evan Gilchrist, who used to be at Atayahuanco with us.'

There was a silence. Looking up, Leigh saw the two men exchange glances, Greg's brows lifting in interrogation, then snapping together in a heavy frown as he absorbed whatever unspoken message he had received from Rourke.

After a pause, he said, 'Well, I sure hope you find him soon.'

The words were polite, but at the same time loaded, Leigh thought as she finished her coffee. She got the strong impression that the story of Evan's disappearance was not news to Greg Mayhew, and that he regarded the younger man's hunt for lost treasure with the same disfavour as Rourke himself. But why?

She felt an ache of compassion for Evan so doggedly and single-mindedly pursuing his dream— with not the slightest idea it was in vain. The sooner she could catch up with him and be totally honest with him the better. Perhaps if he had found some ancient Inca gold, it would soften the blow a little. At least, she hoped so.

Greg was speaking again. 'Now, Leigh, as your medical adviser, I recommend an early night for you. Carlota will show you where you're to sleep.' He smiled at her. 'I apologise again for the primitive arrangements, but Rourke assures me you're accustomed to far worse.'

A protest about being so blatantly bundled out of the way was hovering on the tip of Leigh's tongue, but she bit it back. Clearly the two of them had private matters to discuss, she thought bitterly.

The store room was small, with a single, barred window high in one wall. A space had been cleared on the floor, and two thickly woven straw mats placed there at a discreet distance from each other. A small lamp was glowing gently on top of a pile of wooden boxes.

Leigh chose the mat nearest the window, and lay down, removing nothing but her slippers. Carlota had not offered her any kind of nightwear, and judging by the roguish twinkle in her eyes as she bade Leigh *'Buenas noches'*, she had clearly decided that as the night would be spent in lovemaking, such refinements were unnecessary.

If only she knew, Leigh thought, turning on to her stomach, and pillowing her head on her folded arms. There was far more to separate Rourke and herself than a simple space between two mats, as he had made plain on their journey here. The barrier of silence had been imposed once more with a vengeance. He had appeared wrapped in his own thoughts, practically oblivious of her presence, returning monosyllabic answers to any tentative conversational overtures she had made.

It was obvious he regretted those all too brief moments of lovemaking. 'Madness', he had called them, and perhaps he had been right, but sanity was so cold.

Leigh shivered, biting her lip. Her body ached for the fulfilment it had been so brutally denied, the intensity of her frustration almost shocking. In the past, she had always been so totally in control, or so she had thought. Now she knew that was only an illusion. Before Rourke came into her life, she had only scratched the surface of experience, she realised wearily. Now, quite explicitly, she had been made aware that she was a woman with all a woman's needs.

But though Rourke had aroused those needs, she had to face the fact that he was not obliged to satisfy them, and his whole forbidding attitude to her emphasised this.

She shifted restlessly, wondering once again about the unknown Isabella, and the 'lesson' Rourke had learned from her. It must, she supposed dolefully, have been a potent one if his subsequent reactions were anything to go by. In her mind's eye, she saw a dark-eyed Spanish beauty, all voluptuous arrogance, with a flower in her hair. The kind of woman who met fire with fire, whose passion would be unforgettable, making all other women pale into insignificance beside her.

Particularly, Leigh thought with a sigh, spoiled brats of English girls, who had never been more than a nuisance from the beginning.

She began to sigh again, then determinedly turned it into a yawn. If she continued with this train of thought, she would become thoroughly depressed. In spite of her annoyance at being sent off to bed like an unruly child, there was no denying that she was tired. It had been a long and difficult day, but everything would seem better after a good night's sleep.

She closed her eyes, deliberately relaxing each limb and muscle, and eventually she must have succeeded, because when next she opened her eyes with a little start, the lamp had burned right down, and a glance at her watch in its fading light told her that several hours had passed. And she was still alone, the neighbouring mat unoccupied.

Last night, she had slept in his arms. Tonight, he couldn't even bear to be in the same room with her, she thought restively.

She sat up, pushing her hair out of her eyes, and as she did so, she heard the music.

Wide awake now, she listened intently. She could hear the throb of a drum, then, as if in answer, the soft wail of high-pitched pipes.

Of course, Greg had said there was to be a fiesta. She had intended to ask about it over supper, but the opportunity had never arisen. Now, it seemed, the festivities had begun, but she was being excluded from them as from everything else. 'Well, that's what they think,' she muttered to herself, as she rummaged through her ill-used shoulder bag for a comb. She found other things, too, that she had entirely forgotten about during the last crowded days and nights. A lipstick for one thing, and a purse-size phial of scent—her favourite *Amazone*. She grimaced slightly, as she removed the cap, and the familiar fragrance drifted to her nostrils. She had worn it that night in Lima, but not since, finding it all too evocative of things best forgotten, but now, almost dreamily, she allowed a fine mist of scent to cling to her hair and skin, and touched the new vulnerability of her mouth's curve with colour.

If I'm going to gatecrash a party, she told herself with desperate gaiety, then I may as well do it in style.

The rest of the building seemed empty, the once crowded verandah deserted.

Once in the street, Leigh allowed the sound of the music to guide her towards the square. When she reached the end of the alley, she paused in the shadows for a while.

There was a slip of a new moon in the sky, but its radiance could not compete with the light from the fires which had been kindled in each of the square's corners. In between the fires, in serried ranks, the villagers were seated quietly.

For a fiesta, it was a pretty muted affair, Leigh thought with astonishment. Or were they waiting in silence for it to begin, perhaps? There was an almost tangible sense of anticipation in the air that somehow went deeper than mere excitement. Leigh felt her own scalp tingle in response.

She looked around, and saw Greg and Rourke standing together a few yards away, their backs turned to her. Summoning all her courage, she went over and tapped Greg on the arm.

'Good evening,' she said with a fair attempt at nonchalance. 'I seem to have mislaid my invitation.'

Rourke said levelly, 'I looked in on you a little earlier, but you were asleep.'

'You could have woken me.' She kept her voice light.

He shrugged. 'I thought you needed your rest.' His voice was brusque, but the glance he shot her was revealing, edged with trouble. *Or perhaps I didn't trust myself.* The thought reached her as clearly as if he had spoken it aloud.

She could see him standing over her, watching her in sleep's abandonment. She could feel his hand reaching out to her, then withdrawing at the last moment. Perhaps it was some subconscious sense of deprivation which had woken her.

She wrenched herself back to reality. 'Isn't this rather a dull party?' Deliberately she made her tone flippant.

'It's quite a serious occasion,' Greg said quietly. 'I'm sorry if you were expecting a carnival—dancing in the streets.'

'Isn't it usual?'

'Oh, there'll be dancing,' Rourke confirmed. 'But much later. What happens first is a kind of ritual. There've been a couple of bad harvests, and they want to make some powerful magic to ensure it doesn't happen again.'

The drum was sounding again, with its insistent rhythm, and this time, as well as the pipes' response, Leigh heard the poignant ripple of a harp like a wind sighing, and she saw the waiting crowd sway to the music. She looked round for the musicians, but they were well concealed, adding to the potency and mystery of the sounds they made.

Which was probably the intention, she thought, then tensed as a man's voice, tuneless and pleading, came out of the shadows. *'O, condorcito,'* it wailed. *'O, condorcito.'*

Every hair on the nape of Leigh's neck lifted. She said under her breath, 'What's that?'

'That's the *curandero,'* Rourke told her softly. 'The town's wise man, summoning the spirit of the condor.'

'And will it come?' She felt breathless.

'Yes, it will come.' He was almost whispering. 'It will come to fight and overcome the spirit of the bull, and regain the power of their ancestors.'

She noticed they were alone, Greg having moved to another part of the square.

She said stiltedly, 'I'm sorry. Did my questions annoy him?'

He considered the matter gravely, 'No, but he's very involved in this—more than a mere spectator. These are his people, or that's the way he sees it, so this is his magic too.'

'You said the condor would come to fight a bull—you don't mean a real animal?'

'At one time it would have been,' he said drily. 'And there'd have been a real condor tied to its back, so they could fight it out—the spirit of the Inca against the power of the *conquistador.'*

Leigh shivered, wrapping her arms across her body. 'How cruel!'

'It's a cruel country,' he said. 'Don't pretend you haven't discovered that for yourself.' His voice was almost derisive.

She said unevenly, 'Don't—please. I'm trying to learn. I want to know. . .'

'What do you want to know?' His hand was on her shoulder suddenly, his fingers digging into the skin exposed by the wide neckline of her blouse.

'Everything,' she told him, her gaze meeting his. 'The cruelty as well. I'm not afraid, Rourke. You have to believe that.' She stopped abruptly, wondering what on earth had made her say such a thing. She hadn't consciously formed the words at all, or considered their implications.

'Aren't you afraid, Leigh—aren't you?' The topaz eyes were glittering as they looked into her own. 'But the night—this night of the condor isn't over yet.'

There was a long, harsh sigh from the waiting people, and a man sprang into the firelit square. He was almost naked, his only covering some form of loincloth, and his face was completely concealed by the elaborately constructed mask and face of a huge bull.

The drum's rhythm was paramount now, filling the air as the bull-man pranced and strutted, and pawed at the ground, his movements forceful and ponderous.

All the crushing might of the Spanish conquest seemed encapsulated in the powerful thrusting movements of that grotesquely oversized head, the destructively stamping feet.

The chanting voice came again, *'O condorcito'*, and this time the crowd echoed the sound in a full-throated roar. The bull-man stopped, shoulders hunched, the great head turning from side to side, questing, as if preparing to charge. In spite of herself, Leigh felt the breath catch in her throat.

And then the condor was there, facing him so swiftly and suddenly that it might have dropped from the skies. The face mask was beaked and awesome. Great, trailing black feathered wings attached to the man's arms gleamed blue-black in the firelight as the dancer began to move, turning and swirling, wings dipping at one moment, raised on high at the next.

They must weigh a ton, Leigh thought, fascinated. Yet he was so graceful, so totally in control, obeying every ripple of the harp whose music now filled the listening square.

The bull was moving again too, pawing at the ground, the horned head swinging in menace.

They were both dancers, it was all make-believe, but as the bull charged Leigh cried out, completely caught up in the fantasy. The condor side-stepped the charge, the sweeping wings as taunting as some bull-fighter's cape.

As the bull charged again, Leigh gasped. 'That was close!'

'It was meant to be,' Rourke murmured against her ear. 'The battle is a real one, which the condor must win if the magic is to succeed. Condor dancers have ended up being badly gored by those horns, but that beak can do some damage too.'

She should be shocked. She should walk away in disgust, but it was impossible. She was riveted to the spot, hardly breathing, her eyes fixed on the two masked figures as they circled each other. She could see the trickles of sweat running down their backs and chests, hear, in the intent atmosphere, the rasp of their breathing, as they leaped and ran and turned.

'How long can they keep it up?' she asked, half under her breath.

'Until it's over,' he said. 'Each time I've seen it danced, it's been different.'

Time, Leigh found, became irrelevant. The drama, the mystery of the occasion had her in thrall completely. It was unreal, she thought, that she should be

here watching what amounted to a duel between two
primeval forces. The smoke from the bonfires was
making her eyes water, the breath was thick in her
chest as if she was the condor dancer, evading the
fierce rushes of the opponent, those lethal, seeking
horns.

They were getting tired, she thought feverishly.
They had to be. And as if in confirmation, suddenly
one of the bull's horns struck a glancing blow against
one of the taunting, swirling wings, catching the condor man off balance, and flinging him down into the
dust, bringing a concerted groan from the watching
crowd which Leigh found herself echoing.

No dance, however it turned out, could guarantee
a successful harvest, especially in this kind of climate, and she knew it with Western rationality. But
she also knew the power of positive and negative
thought—knew the watching *campesinos* needed a
sign that there was hope—that nature's forces were
on their side.

The bull-man was gathering himself for the final
charge, head tossing in triumph.

Leigh's hands were balled into fists, her nails digging into her soft palms.

'Oh, get up,' she thought. 'For God's sake get up!'

It was only when she felt Rourke's hands tighten
on her shoulders that she realised she had spoken
aloud.

The condor-man was motionless, the proud wings
tossed and dusty, the harp music barely whispering
now, the drum throbbing victoriously.

But as the bull-man ran, the condor moved, rolling sideways with an incredible burst of new energy,
and now it was the other dancer's turn to be in trouble, stumbling under the impetus of his headlong

charge at his elusive opponent. As he fell forward, the
condor was upon him, both feet planted on his back,
as he lay spreadeagled and helpless in the middle of
the square.

The villagers were on their feet, the atmosphere
was electric. As the great wings lifted slowly and cer-
emoniously above the dancer's head in victory, Leigh
found there were tears on her face.

Rourke turned her slowly to look at him. 'No more
tears, *mi corazón.*' There was an odd note in his voice.
'Now the celebration can begin.'

The music had changed, the slow ritualised beat
giving way to something infinitely more ligh-
thearted, a jogging, foot-tapping melody. And the
villagers were responding to its invitation. The square
was full of movement and colour, men in brightly
coloured ponchos, women in spectacular shawls and
embroidered skirts, many of them carrying babies
strapped to their backs as they danced.

Rourke took Leigh's hands, drawing her forward
into the throng. His smile was teasing, but the
expression in the topaz eyes was serious, and Leigh's
breath caught in her throat as she encountered his
gaze. For a moment she was tempted to pull herself
free, and run to whatever form of safety offered,
because there was nothing ahead of her but heartbreak if she went into Rourke's arms.

Perhaps the primitive form of magic they had just
witnessed had worked some kind of spell on him too,
she thought, as they began to move together to the
music, their hands clasping each other's waists.

Rourke wanted her—his eyes had told her that—
but it was a transitory desire. If she gave herself to
him on this strange magical night of the condor,
might he not turn away from her again when morning came? And could she bear it if he did?

But the argument was already lost, and she knew it. The spell of this night was too strong, catching them together in an inescapable dream. A dream from which she would wake when she had to. Not before, she thought recklessly as he drew her closer, his hands warm and compelling through the thin material of her blouse. She touched him in turn, flattening her palms on the strong, muscular planes of his back, a smile tilting the corners of her mouth as she felt his hips grind against hers in involuntary response.

His brows lifted in mock reproof, and he began to drop tiny, tantalising kisses on her face, his lips caressing her temples, her eyelids, her cheekbones, and the tip of her nose, but deliberately avoiding her eagerly parted lips.

She wanted his mouth on hers more than she had ever wanted anything in the world. This teasing denial was driving her crazy, and he knew it, and the shared knowledge was in some strange way a delight, and a promise. Leigh twined her arms round his neck, letting her fingers tangle in the thick dark hair that grew down on his nape. On this night, for the first and last time, she could touch him in any way she wanted, let her fingertips express the love and need she dared not utter.

His own hands were stroking down her spine, tracing the delicate divide between her shoulder blades, making her body arch towards him so that the points of her uptilted breasts grazed the hard wall of his chest. She was dry-mouthed with excitement, her hands sliding down over his shoulders to discover the swift race of his heart. They were in the centre of the crowd now, hardly able to move for the press of laughing, jigging people around them, but they could have been alone, the shared dream enclosing them.

Rourke lifted his head, and looked down at her, gravely, questioningly. He saw the answer in her eyes, and, holding her clamped possessively to his side, began to fight his way through the throng of dancers to the dark opening of the street which led back to Greg's house.

The lamp was out, and now there was only the pale glimmer of moonlight in the small room, mingling with the muted sound of music from the square.

She was trembling as she watched him close the door. Trembling when he came to her.

He said quietly, 'Are you afraid of me?'

'No.' It was the truth. It was her own inexperience she feared, the possiblility that she might disappoint him. 'But, Rourke, I don't. . . I've never. . .'

His fingers stroked her hair, lifting the dark tawny strands away from the nape of her neck so that he could caress the sensitive skin beneath. 'I know. Trust me, *querida.*'

'With my life,' she whispered. She wrapped her arms round him, burying her face almost fiercely in his chest, breathing in the warm male scent of him. He held her close, and she felt his lips on her hair, then he lifted her gently and put her down on one of the thick straw mats, coming down to lie beside her, his arms cradling her against him.

Gradually, as he held her, Leigh found the shaking, inner tension draining out of her. She lifted a hand and stroked his cheek, running her fingertips over the faint stubble on his jaw.

There was a faint note of laughter in his voice. 'I shaved—with Greg's apology for a razor.'

'Yes,' she acknowledged shyly. Her eyes were fixed on his mouth, her finger tracing its firm outline. He bit the errant finger very gently, and she felt a tiny shock of pleasure transfix her.

He began to caress her slowly, his hand smoothing the line of her throat, and the curve of her shoulder, and she moved restlessly, wanting more, her lips parting in a silent plea to be kissed.

His arms were fierce suddenly, gathering her to him, as his lips took possession of hers. She responded mindlessly, her urgency matching his as they explored each other's moist inner sweetness.

His hand was warm and heavy against her breast, his fingers strumming the aroused, hardening peak. Leigh made a little sound in her throat, and he lifted his head, staring down at her for an endless moment, while he untied the drawstring which fastened her blouse, and pushed the encumbering fabric from her shoulders.

With a sigh of satisfaction, Rourke began to kiss her bared breasts, his tongue languorously circling each heated, taut pink nipple in turn. Leigh gasped at the sensation, her head turning wildly from side to side.

'Leigh, my beautiful one, my honey-flower,' His voice was unsteady as he whispered against her skin. 'I need to taste all your sweetness.'

She felt him dispense with the fastenings at the waistband of her skirt, then lift her slightly so that he could rid her completely of its heavy folds, the loosened blouse following it into oblivion.

His lips trailed fire between her breasts, down over her abdomen to the final lace-trimmed barrier. Her whole body shivered with anticipation and longing as, gently, he began to free her from this final restriction, but some of her former apprehension was flooding back too. She wasn't ashamed of her body, but she had never been completely naked with a man before and—well, she just hadn't, that was all.

Rourke's lips touched hers with infinite gentleness. 'Why have you closed your eyes?'

'I don't know.' She could feel the colour burning up into her face, and hoped the moonlight would conceal the fact.

There was a smile in his voice. 'So, the beautiful sophisticate I met in Lima was all a sham. *Ay de mi!*'

Leigh turned her face into his shoulder. 'But you knew that already.' Her voice was muffled.

'*Sí.* He took her hand and carried it to his lips, then gently tipped her head back, making her look at him. Then he took the heavy gold signet ring he wore on his little finger and slid it gently on to her left hand. 'Is this enough covering for you?'

She stared at him, unable to speak, a deep wellspring of joy bubbling up inside her, and he smiled into her eyes. Then, slowly and gently, his hand moved, making an unhurried sweep of her nude body from shoulder to thigh, and lingering, making the breath catch in her throat.

He kissed her sensuously, his tongue exploring the contours of her mouth, his hands paying homage to the silken core of her womanhood, until her whole body was quivering in abandonment. Her entire being seemed to be drawn into some trembling spiral of need that she had never dreamed could exist, and she buried her face in his throat, her teeth grazing his skin as she tried to stifle her little imploring moans for release.

The caressing fingers altered their rhythm, slightly, subtly, tightening the spiral inside her so unbearably that she cried out sharply, half in fear, half in exultation. Then, incredibly, the tension snapped into a thousand ripples of sensation, spreading through her, reaching a pulsating climax, then receding slowly, leaving her boneless and pliant in his arms.

Huskily, slumbrously, she said at last, 'I—do not believe that.'

'Yet it happened,' Rourke told her softly. 'And that is only the beginning.' He captured her hands and carried them to the fastenings of his own clothes. 'Now, help me, *querida*.'

All inhibitions flown, she did as he asked, letting her fingers explore every inch of his lean, hard-muscled body with the same intimacy that he had shown her, savouring the soft groans of pleasure that her caresses drew from him.

'*Dios,* Leigh,' he muttered at last, his voice hoarse and ragged. 'I need to be gentle with you, but my control isn't endless.'

'Nor is mine,' she admitted shakily, as his hands shaped her breasts, teasing the hard peaks between thumb and forefinger, making her body clench in violent sensation.

Gently, he pressed her back on the straw mat, parting her slim legs so he could kneel between them. The caressing hands were urgent now, passionately demanding, so that she cried out, her body arching towards him, inviting his possession. She saw him poised above her, and gasped, because for a moment his face was a stranger's, sensual and ruthless.

Then as he entered her, all coherent thought faded in the sheer wonderment of this joining of bodies. There was no pain, only a sense of total completion as if she had been created for this moment alone.

He began to move inside her, slowly at first, then more forcefully, and she mirrored his thrusts, their mouths and bodies locked together in heated delight.

Suddenly she heard him call her name as if it had been dredged up from the bottom of his soul, and as

he shuddered wildly against her, her own body con-
vulsed into spasms of pleasure so intense she thought
she would be torn apart.

Afterwards, they lay drained, totally languid in
each other's arms, while he murmured to her softly
in Spanish.

'I wish I knew what you were saying.' Leigh kissed
his shoulder.

'I'll translate for you one day.' He stroked the
sweat-dampened hair back from her face. 'When you
don't blush quite so easily.'

'Perhaps I'll never blush again.'

'I think I can promise that you will.'

'How can you be so sure?' she asked, then, hastily,
'No, don't answer that.' She was silent for a moment.
'They're still dancing in the square.'

'They'll dance until they drop.' He kissed her. 'Do
you, perhaps, wish to join them?'

Leigh stretched, boneless as a cat. 'Oh, I'm quite
content where I am,' she assured him. 'But don't let
me spoil your plans for the rest of the night.'

He gathered her closer. 'Oh, I'm occasionally prepared to sacrifice my own pleasures.'

'A born martyr!' She had imagined herself satisfied, sated even, but now, as his hand began to stroke
her skin again, she felt a swift stir of response.

She thought, I don't believe this either. Then she
ceased to think at all.

CHAPTER EIGHT

LEIGH awoke smiling, and reached for him, only to find she was alone. She sat up slowly, pushing back her hair, and looking round her, conscious of a deep pang of disappointment. She had fallen asleep, eventually, in Rourke's arms. She had expected to wake in his embrace too.

In the sunlight which poured through the single window, the store-room looked even smaller and more cluttered than it had the previous night. It was the least likely setting for a night of passion that Leigh could ever have envisaged. And she had shared it with a man whom she had known for days rather than weeks, she reminded herself. It should have been sordid, but instead it had been the most beautiful thing that had ever happened to her—beautiful and wonderful and—right.

She basked in the sun for a while, coming to terms with the unfamiliar aches and pains, the slight tendernesses which Rourke's lovemaking had engendered. It was only to be expected, she thought, touching herself consideringly. He had been infinitely skilful over her initiation, but as the night went on they had both become oblivious of everything but their need for each other, and the immediate and shattering response the lightest caress could ignite.

Leigh looked wonderingly down at herself. This was the body she had fed, clothed and bathed, and taken totally for granted. Now a whole new facet of her nature—one that she had never dreamed existed—had been revealed to her. The cool façade she had believed in and presented to the world was shattered for ever now, and she didn't regret its passing for an instant.

She touched the soft gleam of Rourke's signet ring with fingers that shook a little. Oh, why wasn't he here, holding her, reassuring her that they belonged together in every way there was? There was so much she wanted to say to him that she hadn't been able to find words for before. There was so much she wanted to hear him say. She needed, she realised slowly, to hear him say that he loved her.

She shivered suddenly and sat up, looking round for her clothes, but there was no sign of the skirt and blouse she had been wearing the previous evening.

She would have to find something to wear, she thought, frowning a little. She wanted a shower and something to eat.

As the store-room door began to open, she gasped and looked round for cover, then relaxed again when she saw it was Rourke. She stretched slightly, and smiled at him, her whole body innocently provocative. 'Good morning,' she said softly.

'*Buenos días.* His voice was curt. 'I've brought you some clothes.'

There were jeans, she saw, and a shirt, clearly brand new.

'Thank you.' She had to resist an urge to snatch them from him, and hold them in front of her like a protective shield. She was being ridiculous, after all. Only a few hours before, his mouth and hands had known every inch of her. But the lover who had given her that first, devastating lesson in sensuality seemed to have vanished in the harsh light of day, to be replaced by some sombre stranger.

She said, 'Rourke, is something wrong?'

'On the contrary, I have some good news for you.' He put the little pile of garments down on an upturned crate making not the least attempt to approach her more closely. 'Greg made radio contact with Atayahuanco at first light. It seems your fiancé has returned, safe and sound.'

Leigh's lips moved stiffly. 'Evan—Evan's at Atayahuanco?'

'And waiting impatiently for your reunion, I understand,' he said. 'Smile then, *querida*. It's what brought you to Peru, after all. And don't look so stricken,' he added cynically. 'I don't—kiss and tell, if that is worrying you.'

'Don't you care?' Desperately, she grabbed the clothes and began to huddle them on.

'On the contrary, I am very happy for you,' he returned courteously.

'I didn't mean that.' She lifted her hand. 'Last night you gave me this.' She touched his ring.

His brows lifted. 'So I did. My profoundest regrets, *querida*. It was a joke—in rather poor taste. Last night was an interlude—enjoyable, of course, but nothing more, provoked by the moonlight and the music, and on my part by too much *chicha*.'

'I see.' The golden bubble of joy and love and physical contentment which had enclosed her since she opened her eyes had shattered into a thousand dull fragments. She hadn't known it was possible to feel such pain. She wrenched the ring over her knuckle and held it out to him. 'You'd better have it back. It's obviously old, and valuable.'

'I should hate to lose it.' Rourke let her drop it into his palm. 'We can leave as soon as you are ready.'

'I'll try not to keep you waiting. But I'd be grateful for a wash—and a comb.'

'I'll send Carlota to you,' he said, and the door closed behind him.

Alone, Leigh wrapped her arms across her body, moaning softly at the agony that was tearing her apart. She was ashamed, as well as wretched, ashamed of the unstinted giving, of her own feverish demands. Ashamed of the naïveté which had deluded her into thinking that their lovemaking had been any more to him than a convenient sexual release.

Now, for the first time, she wanted to run—away from this place, away from Atayahuanco, away from Lima—oh God, away from this whole harsh, beautiful country to the safety of home.

It was, after all, what he had urged her to do all along, she thought painfully. But she had been so sure of herself, so certain of her destination, and the motives which took her there. There were no more certainties now.

But she had to go on with it. She had to complete the journey to Atayahuanco, and meet up with Evan again, if only to tell him it was all over between them.

She found herself wondering incuriously if she had ever really loved him at all, or if their relationship had simply been nurtured by her family's hostility towards him, and her reaction against that.

She bit her lip. How selfish she had been, what a monster of ego to condemn Evan to this year of misery—and for nothing. She dreaded having to face him, having to attempt some halting explanation about this amazing change of heart. What, after all, could she say? At best, it would have to be half-truths.

'I'm no longer the girl you knew in England,' she would have to say. 'I've changed utterly. It wouldn't work any more.'

What she could never say was, 'I belong to another man. What I always denied you, I gave and gave again to him.' Nor the sad postscript: 'But he no longer wants me.'

A shudder tore through her, then another. There were beads of sweat on her face, and her hands were tightly clenched as she fought for self-control. Life goes on. Since she was a small child, she had heard her father saying that buoyantly, bracingly when some crisis, major or trivial, had been weathered. At times, the expression had irritated her. Now it seemed something to cling to.

She was relatively calm when she entered the tiny dining-room to find Greg Mayhew wading through an immense plateful of fried potatoes, topped with a fried egg.

'Sit down. Have some coffee.' He began to fill a beaker from an enamel pot in the centre of the table. 'Rourke's gone to see to the mule,' he added, correctly interpreting her swift, sideways glance round the room. 'Carlota will bring you some food in a minute.'

'I'm not very hungry.'

He shrugged. 'Even so, you should eat something. In our part of Paradise, you never know where your next hot meal is coming from. Or haven't you noticed?'

She drank some coffee. It was black and bitter, but she could feel it putting heart into her, and she was grateful for that.

'You'd better let me take a look at that foot of yours before you leave,' he went on.

'Oh, I think it's fine,' she said hurriedly. 'I was actually dancing on it last night.'

'But not for long,' he said gently, and Leigh felt hot colour rush into her face.

'You don't approve?' She lifted her chin challengingly.

'I try not to make judgements. Women with your looks and style are as rare as flying fish up here. I guess if I'd been in Rourke's shoes, I'd have grabbed for whatever was on offer too.' He paused.

'And your own guy's waiting for you at Atayahuanco, so there's no permanent harm done.'

Leigh took another mouthful of coffee. Her voice steady, she asked, 'Who is Isabella?'

He grimaced. 'My big mouth, eh? I spend so much time shouting at the *campesinos* about their kids' shots, and elementary hygiene, I sometimes forget to keep my voice down.'

She shook her head. 'She's been mentioned before.'

'I see.' There was a brief silence. Then, 'Isabella is the girl Rourke intended to marry.'

'Past tense?'

'Very much so,' he said with emphasis. 'As a matter of fact, the whole thing was pretty much of a disaster.'

'Was she a—a Peruvian girl?'

'Hell, no, she was an American. Her real name was Isabel, but Rourke like to pretty it up. They met at some diplomatic shindig in Washington, and he fell hard. They were engaged in weeks. On the face of it, it seemed an ideal match. They came from the same background, both families were loaded, and she looked like every man's fantasy woman. Then he took her to Atayahuanco, and it all began to come unstuck.' He shook his head. 'She just wasn't ready for that at all.'

'What was the problem?'

'What wasn't?' Greg shrugged again, frowning. 'I guess she'd misread the entire situation. She thought Peruvian Quest was just a job, a stage in Rourke's career. She couldn't or wouldn't accept that it was his whole life. She tried like hell to talk him out of it—got her father to pull strings so that he'd be made all kinds of job offers. She just couldn't see that he'd dedicated a piece of his life to the Quechua, and that there was no way he was going to renege on that. And when talking didn't work, she threw a scene a minute. Only that didn't work either.'

'What happened in the end?' Leigh drained her beaker, and Greg re-filled it.

'They shipped her out, back to Washington. In the fullness of time, she married a corporation lawyer, which was probably the best thing that could have happened.'

'But he still cares for her.' The words weren't easy to say.

'Well, you don't just write off something like that.' Greg pushed his empty plate away. 'She was going to be part of his life. Her problem was she wanted to be all of it, and that wouldn't work for Rourke—or for me either. Which is why we stay single.'

'With the occasional diversion.' Leigh managed to keep her voice steady.

'It works both ways.' He leaned back in his chair. 'When you're a settled married lady, you'll be able to take out your memories and dust them off occasionally. That can be no bad thing—as long as you don't dwell in the past.'

And if the past is all there is, she thought, what happens when there is no future?

Aloud, she said, 'Thanks for the word of warning. I presume that's what it was.'

'Read it how you like.' He gave her a steady look. 'You don't belong here, Miss Frazier, any more than Isabel Crofton Barnes did. Just be glad you're getting out with no bones broken—on either side.'

How could he say that, she wondered numbly when every part of her was shattered into tiny, hurting fragments? He was crediting her with the kind of sophistication she had always used as a façade, a shield to hide behind—a shield, she now saw, was her only means of salvation.

Carlota brought a plate heaped with food, and Leigh made a passable attempt to eat it, turning the conversation to the clinic and the work there, listening to the problems of malnutrition and lack of hygiene which Greg had to deal with every day.

'The conditions are the same at Atayahuanco, aren't they?' she asked, and he nodded.

'If anything they're worse, because the Quechua who still live in the valley there have been cut off from even basic civilisation for quite some time, and they've deteriorated pretty badly. It's amazing people who have so little can survive at all.'

'And that's why Peruvian Quest is there,' she said. 'Trying to revive the ancient crafts and skills, trying to restore their pride in themselves.'

She saw faint surprise in his face. 'How did you figure that out?'

'It didn't take much figuring. After all, much of the financing for the project comes from my father's companies. Or didn't Rourke mention that?'

'No,' he said, after a thoughtful pause. 'I guess it must have slipped his mind.'

When she had finished her meal, he took her into the surgery, and re-dressed her foot, swiftly and deftly.

'No sign of infection there,' he commented with satisfaction. He shot her an old-fashioned look. 'Keep off the dance floor for a day or two, and you should be as good as new.'

She managed a nonchalant shrug. 'Oh, I shan't be doing any more dancing.'

'I'm glad to hear it.' He rested a large hand momentarily on her shoulder, his face and voice softening a little. 'You'll do, Leigh Frazier.'

There was still no sign of Rourke, and she had no idea where he had pastured the mule for the night, so after a brief hesitation she walked up to the square, and stood looking about her.

In the harsh sunlight, it was like another world, last night's fires reduced to piles of ash, the excited throng replaced by a few women squatting on the pavements selling a few, pitiful handfuls of vegetables. No moonlight, no magic, no primitive life-force struggle to carry her away this morning.

Reality had returned with a vengeance. The night of the condor was over.

It was late afternoon when they reached Atayahuanco. Rourke had set a gruelling pace, sparing neither of them, and in a way Leigh was glad of it. It meant she had to apply all her concentration to the sheer physical effort of keeping up with him, so that there was no time to think, or brood. She carried her unhappiness inside her, cold and heavy like a stone.

She looked almost incuriously down at the valley she had battled so hard and so far to reach, for all the wrong reasons.

On the opposite hillside, she could see the remains of the old agricultural terraces and irrigation channels, and high above them the tumbled stones of the excavation, the citadel rearing proudly to challenge the surrounding peaks.

Immediately below her, at a short distance from the stream which meandered through the valley bottom she saw the Peruvian Quest encampment of tents and prefabricated buildings, and tiny figures moving between them. One of whom would be Evan, she thought, biting her lip.

There was no possible retreat. She didn't need Rourke's laconic, 'They've seen us,' to tell her their arrival had been noted below. Bracing herself, she began the steep descent towards the camp.

Fergus Willard was the first to greet them, a tall bony man with a pleasant, worried face. He grasped Rourke's hand, and they exchanged a few words in an undertone, before he turned to Leigh.

'Well, Miss Frazier.' His voice was rather too hearty. 'So you actually made it. That's amazing!'

She smiled charmingly, very much her father's daughter in spite of clothes which fitted where they touched. 'I had an excellent guide.'

'Er—yes, of course.' Doctor Willard's face told her plainly that he found this the most amazing thing of all. 'No one knows this terrain like Rourke, after all.' He put up his hand and pulled at his greying beard. 'Rourke will have told you, naturally, that Gilchrist has returned.' He smiled nervously. 'It must be a great relief for you. You must be anxious to see him again.'

Leigh was searingly aware that Rourke was watching her, could feel his eyes on her as surely as if he had reached out and touched her with his hand. She lifted her chin. 'Yes—most anxious.'

'Well, I'll just show you where you'll be spending the night first,' Dr Willard said. 'I've arranged for you to share a tent with our other ladies—we've just moved another bed in.' He frowned slightly. 'It's rather cramped, but as it's only for a very short time, we thought you might be prepared to make the best of it.'

Leigh smiled again. 'I'm sure it will be fine.' She paused. 'But I have no plans to dash away immediately, Doctor Willard. I'm sure my father and his board would appreciate a first-hand report on everything that's happening here.'

The consternation was almost tangible.

At last Doctor Willard said heavily. 'I see. Well, we'll do our best to accommodate you, Miss Frazier, but our resources are limited.'

'Don't worry about a thing,' she told him airily. 'I've grown quite accustomed to that over the past few days.'

Fergus Willard shrugged resignedly, and turned to lead the way into the camp.

Leigh made to follow him, but Rourke's hand closed on her arm detaining her.

'What new game is this?' His mouth was compressed, a tiny betraying muscle flickering in his jaw.

She stared back at him with a calmness she was far from feeling. 'No game at all. Now that I've got here, I intend to stay for a while, that's all.'

He released her curtly. 'You may find your fiancé has other ideas,' he said, and strode off in the opposite direction.

The camp seemed to be a hive of activity, Leigh thought as she followed Fergus Willard. Their route took them through the kitchen area where large pots of stew and vegetables were being stirred over open fires. Naturally, her arrival was receiving a great deal of attention, but the smiles which greeted her, she noted, were on the guarded side of friendly.

When they reached the tent, it was deserted. Looking round her, Leigh saw that Fergus Willard had not exaggerated about the shortage of space.

We shall have to take it in turns to breathe, she thought wryly.

'Well, this is it, Miss—er—Frazier.' Doctor Willard made a vaguely all-encompassing gesture. 'The bed in the corner is yours, and there's a tin chest for your gear. It prevents insects getting into your clothes, or that's the theory anyway.'

'As I only have what I stand up in, that shouldn't be too much of a problem.' Leigh put her shoulder-bag down on the cot he had indicated.

He looked shocked. 'I had no idea—you must feel free to draw whatever you need from the camp store.' He paused. 'Again, I'm afraid it's. . .'

'Rather limited,' Leigh supplied wearily when he hesitated. 'Believe me, Doctor Willard, I'd be glad of anything.'

'I'll get June to have a word with you. As well as being our nurse, she looks after that side of things.' He turned to go, clearly relieved at having disposed of one problem at least. 'And now I'll find Gilchrist for you.' He paused again, and this time there was nothing vague in the look he sent her. 'If I might give you some advice, Miss Frazier, I would get back to Britain just as quickly as you can. It's no longer safe here. Not safe at all.' He gave her a bleak nod, and vanished.

'Darling!' Evan's voice was exultant. 'Oh God, I can hardly believe it!'

Leigh forced a smile. 'Nor can I.' She stepped back, out of the circle of his arms. 'How—how are you, Evan?'

'Better, now that you're here.' He stared at her, his smile fading slightly. 'You look tired, angel, and thinner. Was it a hellish journey? Willard said something about you having no luggage.'

'It was stolen,' she told him. 'And I think anyone would lose weight with the amount of walking I've done this week.'

He looked at her with sudden sharpness. 'Was everything stolen—your money, your passport?'

'No, I still have those.' She touched her bag.

'Thank heaven for that!'

'Amen,' she said rather ironically. 'But why?'

'Because it means there's nothing to stop us leaving this God-forsaken country.' Evan put an arm around her, hugging her. 'You don't know what that means to me!'

Leigh looked down at her bare hands, remembering the golden gleam of Rourke's ring. She said slowly, 'I'm not leaving at once, Evan. I'm staying here for a while.'

'Here?' The incredulity in his face was almost comic. He stared round him. 'You have to be joking, love! You don't know what conditions are like here. You'll be eaten alive by fleas for starters, and every drop of water has to be filtered and treated. And have you seen the latrines yet? They're a nightmare!'

She said drily, 'So you told me in your letters. But it makes no difference. I want to see for myself what's being done here.'

Evan's arm fell away. He said sharply, 'I'll tell you what's being done—a lot of time, money and effort is being wasted on a pack of disease-ridden, fly-blown Indians who are too lazy and apathetic to shift for themselves. I imagine twenty-four hours will tell you all you need to know, and you'll be as glad to get away as I am.'

She still didn't look at him, or let him see how much the venom in his words had shaken her.

'Then why did you come back?'

'To see you, darling.' Hi voice was cajoling again. 'I thought you'd come to tell me my life sentence had been commuted. I thought we'd be leaving together right away.'

Leigh brushed a hand along the coarse denim of her jeans. 'But you didn't know I was coming,' she said in a matter-of-face tone. 'Rourke told me that the radio message was received after you—went off.'

There was a silence. 'Oh, even in this wilderness there's a well established grapevine,' he said at last. 'Any kind of news spreads like wildfire. And I wasn't that far away.'

'Where were you, Evan?' She looked at him directly, noticing how his eyes shifted evasively from hers.

'Treasure-hunting, like I promised.' He looked uneasy and triumphant at the same time, she thought, troubled.

'And you—found some treasure.'

'Oh, yes!' His tone was gloating. 'There's plenty here for everyone, if you know where to look.'

It was very hot in the tent, but in spite of that she shivered. 'Evan—whatever it is you've found, for God's sake put it back before it's too late.'

'Put it back?' He looked at her blankly. 'Are you crazy?'

'I'm trying to be sane for both of us.' Leigh struggled to keep her voice level. 'I don't know what the laws are about archaeological finds, but I imagine they're pretty severe, and the authorities know what you've been doing—why you disappeared like that without a word to anyone.'

'What do you mean?' he demanded harshly.

'Because Rourke said what you'd been doing was criminal, and in Cuzco, the police came to see me. They—frightened me.'

He uttered a violent obscenity, and sat very still, staring ahead of him, lost in some private inner world.

In spite of her uneasiness, Leigh felt sorry for him, and guilty too. After all, it was for her that he had stolen these things—gems, gold, artefacts—whatever they were. She was the princess, to whom he would bring the golden apples. And in the fairy stories, the princess was always waiting, ready to be won, never in any circumstances uncaring or unfaithful, committed body and soul to another man.

She put a hand on his arm. 'Evan, I'm sure if you went to the authorities and explained—told them everything, they'd let you off.'

'With a caution?' He laughed hoarsely. 'God, Leigh you don't know what you're talking about! In this country, they lock you up and throw away the key.' He shook his head. 'No, I'm getting away from here, with or without your help. For the first time in my life I've got the chance to have some money—some real money of my own—more than I've ever dreamed of.'

Leigh got to her feet. All her plans had once been centred on this man, and now he was as much a stranger to her as if they had only met that day.

She said quietly, 'Don't rely on dreams, Evan. They can—distort things. Now, perhaps you'll leave me. I'm rather tired.'

She lay on the cot, with her eyes closed, but she couldn't sleep. The communal evening meal, with all the workers from the camp gathered round one long table swapping stories and experiences from the day, had been the longest she had ever spent. She had sat beside Evan, awkwardly aware that they were distanced from everyone else at the table. Evan had laughed and talked loudly, as if he sensed their isolation, and was trying to deny it, but if that was in fact his intention it was a dismal failure. It merely stressed how very little they were being included in the general conversation. And what had made the situation next door to unbearable had been that Rourke was seated opposite them. Leigh had watched him covertly and almost obsessively under her lashes, her whole being crying out for a look, a smile, some indication at least that she hadn't imagined the passionate lover who had made her part of himself the previous night.

But he didn't so much as glance in her direction. All his attention seemed to be centred on Consuelo Estebán and her black-haired, sullen prettiness.

Leigh had met Consuelo, together with June Muirhead, a much older woman with a strong pleasant face, in the tent when they had come to wash and put on clean shirts before supper. June's attitude had been the warmest Leigh had encountered at Atayahuanco, but perhaps she was just trying to make up for Consuelo's graceless flouncings and mutterings in Spanish. It was quite clear that she bitterly resented having to make room for another girl in the tent, and her treatment of Leigh bordered on the insolent.

'Tantrum time again,' June had observed resignedly when at last Consuelo had taken herself off with another inimical flash of the eyes in Leigh's direction. 'I don't know which would do her the most good—a course of tranquillisers, or an almighty sock on the jaw. I know which I'd prefer to administer,' she added, grinning, and Leigh wasn't disposed to argue with her.

She was grateful to June too for the change of underwear, the towel, and the toilet things which she had presented to her.

'We'll find you some proper boots tomorrow,' June had decreed, casting a critical glance at Leigh's soft leather footwear. 'Those things may be all right when you're on the back of a mule, but they'd be no protection against some of the insects and other wildlife we find round here.'

'I see,' Leigh had said in a hollow voice, and June had laughed again.

'Rourke says we have to look after you,' she said casually, and Leigh's heart leapt.

'Did he?' she managed.

'Sure. Your father's an important benefactor, after all. We can't let any harm come to his only daughter.' June's smile robbed the words of any offence, but Leigh's spirits plummeted again. So that was all he had meant, she thought despondently.

Watching him with Consuelo, it occured to her, painfully, that his decision to place her at arms' length might not have concerned Evan at all. The Spanish girl had suddenly become vivacious, fluttering her admittedly long lashes, wasting no opportunity to brush against him, or touch his sleeve with her small thin hand. He wasn't moving out of range, she thought. Perhaps at Atayahuanco, Consuelo was his woman. After all, she couldn't imagine him living like a monk for months on end. And maybe it was worth more to him to maintain a stable, long-term relationship which would still be there when she, Leigh, had gone back to England, than indulge himself with any number of diversions such as she had represented.

She had thought she knew what it was to be jealous when she had heard about Isabella, but she was wrong. She felt her nails curling into claws. She wanted to lean across the table and wipe that complacent smile from the other girl's face. Her reaction was so savage, so violent that she shocked herself.

And perhaps Consuelo was jealous too, she thought. Maybe that explained the flouncing and hostility.

'Come for a moonlit stroll,' Evan had suggested, his lips against her ear as the meal ended.

Leigh stiffened. 'I'd rather not—I'm still very tired. And I haven't got the right sort of shoes,' she added placatingly, as she saw a sulky expression cross his face.

'Just as you want,' he said, after a pause. 'But we've got to talk, Leigh, and talk seriously.'

She said quietly, 'Yes, I think we should, Evan, but please don't think you're going to persuade me to leave here before I'm ready.' And she walked off before he could voice the protest she could see forming.

Now, as she lay still, trying not to disturb the even breathing of her companions, she found worry about Evan and his problems vying with her wretchedness over Rourke.

In some ways she felt guiltily responsible for what Evan had done, and she would have to live with that. She should have recognised the basic weakness in him when they first met, she thought, recognised it, and eased herself out of the relationship before there was any talk of marriage, before Evan had been thrust into a situation that was beyond him.

She sighed, turning on to her side, and as she did so, became aware of movement in the tent, not from the bed next to her where June slept the sleep of the just, but from the other corner.

Watching through her lashes, she saw Consuelo sit up cautiously, pushing back the shrouding netting, and reach for her boots.

Motionless, Leigh saw the other girl rise, pulling on a robe, and move like a ghost through the crowded tent. Saw her fumble with the flap, and vanish silently into the moonlight.

To Rourke, she thought. To lie in his arms, and know all the passion, all the tenderness that I knew last night.

She took a corner of the coarse pillow and stuffed it into her mouth to stifle the sob welling up inside her. And all the desolate, icy loneliness of the high *sierras* seemed to invade her very soul as she lay in the darkness, and mourned for the love which had never been hers.

CHAPTER NINE

THE Indian woman lying on the straw mat gave a jerk and a shudder, her eyes rolling mutely. Her hands closed on Leigh's wrists with such force that Leigh had to bite back a yelp of pain.

I'm here to provide reassurance, she reminded herself breathlessly, not to start a general panic, although there was enough to panic about.

People who complained about the British National Health Service should be here in the foetid darkness of this stone house, little better than a cave, watching the Quechua woman struggling to bring another life into the world, a situation complicated by the fact that the baby had turned at the last moment and was a breech presentation.

Leigh looked at June Muirhead's calm, composed face, and felt comforted. In the week since she had been at Atayahuanco, she had accompanied June on her rounds each morning, as another pair of hands to obey instructions and pass things, but this was the first emergency she had been faced with, although June had been keeping a close eye on the heavily pregnant woman each day.

'It's lucky we were here,' June remarked prosaically, catching Leigh's eye, and Leigh grinned weakly, wishing she could ease her aching back, or at least push her sweat-soaked hair back from her face. I'll have to tie it back as June does, she thought.

Some of the other women were crouching in the doorway, watching impassively, and incidentally blocking what little natural light filtered into the cramped room, but June made no move to send them away, as Leigh had half expected.

'She needs them there,' she had explained briefly, and that was that.

'Now then,' June said suddenly. The Quechua woman's face contorted, her mouth opening in a silent scream, as June worked furiously, then sat back on her heels smiling as a faint, quavering wail was heard.

'A boy,' June remarked. 'And a fighter, as he'll need to be, poor kid.' She tied off the umbilical cord, cut it, then passed the naked, squirming baby to his mother.

A stronger, more insistent cry came from a straw basket in the corner, and June glanced ruefully in its direction. 'Big sister has woken up,' she said. 'Leigh, take her outside will you, honey, and see if you can keep her quiet. We'll have to try her on some kind of formula later, as I doubt whether Mama has enough milk for two.' She sighed, then added gently, 'Go on, you could do with a rest. I'll clear up here.'

It was bakingly hot outside. Leigh sat down in the dust, leaning back against one of the stone doorposts, the baby cradled in her lap. The mere fact of being picked up seemed to have soothed her to sleep again, Leigh thought, softly brushing away the insistent flies trying to alight on the child's crusted eyelids. It was such an uphill struggle for these children from the moment of birth, and hardly any wonder, as June had told her, that few of them survived those first years.

She closed her eyes against the glare of the sun. Every stitch of clothing she had on was sticking to her. A bath, she thought longingly, or a cool shower.

'So here you are,' a peevish voice said. 'What the hell are you doing?'

'Baby-sitting,' Leigh answered briefly, with an inward groan. She hadn't expected Evan to track her here. Usually he kept as far away from the Quechua settlement as possible.

'Dear God,' he muttered, looking down at the sleeping baby, his face twisted in distaste. 'Doesn't it ever occur to you that you might catch some foul thing from these people?'

'Perhaps I share June's natural immunity,' she said drily. 'I suggest you keep your distance, however.'

'I intend to,' he returned impatiently. 'How much longer are you going on with this charade? I don't know who you're trying to impress with your imitation of Florence Nightingale's right-hand woman, but it gives me no pleasure to see you squatting in the dust like a peasant. You were always so cool and elegant, Leigh. That's the image of you I cherished. What's happened to you?'

'I've changed, Evan.' She settled the baby more comfortably, and looked up at him gravely. 'People do.'

'Not that much,' he insisted almost feverishly. 'Leigh, you don't have to prove anything to me—you know that. You're Justin Frazier's daughter, for God's sake. All you have to do is tell Fergus Willard you've seen enough, and you'll get the VIP treatment out of here—we both will.'

She sighed. 'Evan, how many times must I tell you? I'm not ready to leave yet. But I'm not stopping you doing anything you want.'

'You think I could go, and leave you here?' He sounded almost self-righteous, and she had to bite back a smile. He went on, a martyred note creeping

in. 'Oh, I know you're not in love with me any more—
you've made that more than clear, but you came here
to be with me—to take me out of here, and I'm
counting on you, Leigh.'

'I'm sorry,' she said quietly, after a pause. 'You're
entitled to feel let down, Evan. I—I can't offer any
excuse, except that maybe I know myself a little better now. The girl you knew in England was only half
a person.'

'I don't know what you're talking about,' he muttered angrily. 'The altitude must have got to you—
turned your brain. But if you wanted to break our
engagement, you didn't have to do your dramatic
trek across the *puna*. A letter would have done just as
well.' He gave her a fulminating look and turned
away, plunging down the steep track back towards
the camp.

'Boyfriend trouble?' asked June pleasantly from
the doorway.

'Ex-boyfriend trouble.' Leigh surrendered the
baby into her arms.

'Hm,' June said thoughtfully. 'I can't say I'm
heartbroken to hear it. He's been a pain ever since he
got here, bragging about his connections, throwing
his future father-in-law's name at Fergus, every time
he was asked to do some simple thing. And then—
—' She paused abruptly.

'Yes?' Leigh prompted.

June shrugged, looking deeply uncomfortable.
'Well—disappearing like that, without a word to
anyone.'

Leigh had the strongest impression that wasn't
what June had started out to say.

She said slowly, 'Yes, that was stupid, but it was
partly my fault—a private joke we had going about

him seeking lost treasure to make his fortune.' She shrugged. 'I never dreamed he'd take it so seriously.' She stiffened. 'June, you've got that look on your face!'

'What look is that?' June asked weakly.

Leigh sighed. 'The look everyone gets when Evan's walkabout is mentioned. As if you're all in on some big secret, except me.'

'You're imagining things,' June's tone held its usual robustness. 'When you pull a stunt like that, naturally there are going to be all kinds of rumours, but if Evan told you he was looking for Inca gold, then maybe that's what he was doing.'

Leigh's eyes were fixed on her face. 'But you don't think so?'

June shrugged. 'Honey, I just don't know. But there's more than one sort of treasure round here— if you know where to look.' She paused. 'Why don't you have a chat with Rourke?'

Leigh gave a strained smile. 'Perhaps I will.'

Was it possible, she wondered, that June hadn't noticed that Rourke had addressed barely two words to her all the time she had been at Atayahuanco?Only the previous night, he had arrived late at the supper table. There had been a seat beside her which he had ignored, making room for himself farther down the table, at the opposite side. She had been choked with misery, convinced that everyone had noticed and drawn their own conclusions, but when she looked up from her plate, there were no awkward silences, no pitying looks. Everyone was carrying on with their own lives, and her neighbour was offering her more potatoes. Perhaps they had assumed it was part of the general aloofness he showed to everyone—except presumably Consuelo. He seemed to prefer to spend his moments of relaxation in her company, and Leigh was growing accustomed to the pain of seeing the girl creep out of the tent each night.

It hadn't taken her long to appreciate the admiration and respect in which Rourke was held by his colleagues. He worked untiringly, and no task was too menial for his attention, even though his function on the project was primarily an archaeological one.

And wasn't that why she had been breaking her back ever since she got here, she thought wryly, accepting everything that came her way without complaint, in the hopes of winning perhaps one word of grudging respect from him before they parted for ever.

Or that was how it had begun, at least. Now, to her own surprise, she was caught up in the project on her own account, her interest captured by the small, patient advances June and the rest of the medical team were making; her imagination fired by the Inca and pre-Inca finds being turned up on the dig nearly every day.

She was beginning to understand too why the others on the project had been so wary at first, and June's caustic remarks had confirmed her suspicions.

The name 'Frazier' must have been a dirty word, she thought, grimacing slightly.

'Something wrong?' asked June, as they began to walk back to the camp.

Leigh wriggled her shoulders inside her shirt. 'Just hot—and beginning to crawl, I think.'

June laughed. 'Look, why don't you reward yourself with a visit to what passes for a bathing-pool round here?'

Leigh's eyes widened. 'Is there such a thing?'

'Sure there is. I thought Consuelo had mentioned it to you. She was off there the other day, and I suggested she take you along. You walk upstream, a couple of hundred yards to where the stream deepens. I usually do some laundry at the same time, and hang the stuff on the bushes to dry. Go on, spoil yourself!'

'I think I will.' Leigh wasn't in the least surprised that Consuelo had said nothing. The Peruvian girl made little effort to conceal her hostility. Perhaps her intuition had picked up that Leigh and Rourke had been more than companions on a journey—or maybe Rourke had made a lover's confession, although he had said he didn't kiss and tell, Leigh thought miserably.

'Grab a towel, and get going,' June advised. 'I'll keep the rest of the world at bay for you.'

The pool wasn't difficult to find, and was sufficiently sheltered by bushes and stunted trees to provide some privacy. The stream bed had been hollowed out here, probably by some past flood, to provide a chest-deep bath where the current ran sluggishly.

Mindful of June's advice, Leigh stripped and rinsed out her clothes first, hanging them to dry before lowering herself carefully into the water. She would have loved to have swum, immersing herself totally, but the constant warnings of Jim Holloway and the rest of the medical team about the ever-present danger of dysentery made her wary. So she splashed about gently, enjoying the sensation of the lapping coolness against her overheated flesh, cupping handfuls of water and pouring them over her shoulders and breasts.

She was in the act of wading back slowly to the bank, when she glanced up and saw Rourke, still as a statue, watching her.

How long had he been there? she wondered, her heart thudding painfully. For a moment she almost faltered, then she lifted her head proudly, and continued to walk towards him, her hands nervously flicking the damp tendrils of hair back from her shoulders.

He said hoarsely, 'I'm sorry. I did not realise. . .' and turned, his back rigid and uncompromising, as Leigh pulled herself out of the water and reached for her towel.

As she began to dry herself, she said tightly, 'You have actually seen it all before.'

'I do not need any such reminder,' he threw back at her curtly. 'Under the present circumstances, I would be grateful if you would cover yourself.'

'I'm not putting on damp clothes to appease any sudden rush of prudishness from you,' Leigh said angrily. 'May I ask why you chose to follow me here?'

Rourke said coldly, 'I did not follow you. I was on my way back to camp, when I noticed you in the distance walking alone, in the foolhardy manner which is typical of you.'

'And instead, I'm just taking a foolhardy bath. How disappointing for you!' Leigh wrapped the towel round her, sarong-style, tucking the fold in securely. 'There, I'm decent, if it matters so much.'

He said between his teeth, 'Of course it matters! Doesn't it occur to you that anyone might have come here—might have seen you? Or don't you care? The women usually bathe as a group. Why didn't you ask Consuelo to accompany you?'

Hands shaking, Leigh rearranged some of her laundry. She said, 'As it happens, June guaranteed me some privacy here. As for Consuelo——' She paused, head bent so that her hair obscured her face. 'Do you really think we would choose each other's company?'

There was a tense silence, then he said, 'So you know—I'm sorry.'

'There's really no need to apologise. It was over between us before I even arrived here. I accepted that.'

'Then why do you stay here? Why don't you go back to England before you are hurt again?' He took a step towards her, his face taut and drawn. 'Believe me, Leigh, it would be better if you went now.'

She lifted her chin. 'I'm sorry my presence is so inconvenient for you. Why can't you just go on pretending I don't exist? It's worked very well so far.'

He closed his eyes for a moment. 'It hasn't worked at all, and you know it.'

Leigh said wearily, 'I don't think I know anything any more.' She bit her lip. 'But if I'm an embarrassment, I'll leave. And I'll take Evan with me.' She gave a choked little laugh. 'There—two thorns out of your flesh at once!'

He shook his head slowly, his eyes fixed on her face. 'That—won't be possible.'

She stared at him. 'But that's ridiculous! You don't want him here, and he doesn't want to stay. He's been plaguing me to leave with him ever since I arrived.'

'I wish it were that simple.'

'Why can't it be?' She grabbed a comb out of her bag and began to drag it through her hair, with angry, jerky movements. 'Oh, I see. Evan has to do penance for taking the mule and vanishing like that. Isn't that rather petty?'

'If that were the reason—yes. But it is not.' Rourke's voice was bitter. 'Don't you understand,

Leigh? The matter is no longer in our hands. It is not a question of internal discipline. Now, the police authorities are involved.'

A little wail of distress broke from her. 'Oh, no! But surely you could do something for him—or Doctor Willard? I know he's been a fool, but if he gives back whatever it is he's found, surely they won't be too hard on him?'

He expelled a harsh breath. 'Can you still be so naïve? Can you honestly care for a man who has demonstrated he is worthless in every way?'

Leigh shook her head. 'You're very hard on him. . .'

He said quietly, 'I would like to take him apart with my bare hands. Not just because of the foul trade he has become part of, but because he has put Peruvian Quest in jeopardy. We exist here, Leigh, not merely because of money from Fraziers and other corporations, but with the goodwill of the authorities. Evan Gilchrist has damaged that goodwill badly. Our whole operation will be regarded with suspicion from now on, because of his activities.'

'I didn't realise they were so protective—and I'm sure Evan didn't either. Rourke, he's learned his lesson, I'm sure of it. And he's scared. Don't turn your back on him—please! You could help him.'

'He is beyond anyone's help,' he said harshly. 'It is not just the police, you little fool. He has angered powerful men. Worse things could happen to him than being sent to jail. You wish to see him live out his life, perhaps, without hands or feet?'

'Oh God!' Bile rose in her throat, and she gagged, clammy perspiration breaking out all over her body.

'Dios, querida!' His voice was remorseful, his arms strong, drawing her against the hard shelter of his

body. 'I should not have frightened you—but I have to make you see. . .'

She leaned against him, taking comfort from his strength until the sick trembling began to subside, to be replaced by an even more disturbing sensation. She pressed her face into his shoulder, breathing the warm, male scent, remembering, as slow excitement began to uncurl inside her, how he had taught her, during their night of lovemaking, to use and enjoy every sense she possessed.

His shirt was unfastened almost to the waist, and she lifted her hands, pushing the edges of the deep vee of material even further apart before flattening her palms against his bare chest, testing for herself the mad hurry of his heartbeat which matched her own.

Swiftly, his hands captured her wrists, tugging them away. 'No, *alma mia.*' His voice sounded tortured, his skin drawn tautly over his cheekbones.

But he wanted her. Wickedly Leigh moved her hips sinuously against him, enjoying the physical proof of his urgency that he could neither disguise nor deny. She bent her head, and flicked her small pink tongue provocatively over each flat male nipple in turn.

Rourke groaned, the sound torn from his throat. 'Leigh, you don't know what you're doing!'

'Oh, but I do,' she said softly. 'I had a very good teacher, remember?'

'How could I forget?' he muttered thickly. 'But, *querida,* this is wrong. . .'

'Ah, but it feels so right.' She ran her hands down his back, and over his flanks, revelling in the touch, in the strength of bone, and clenching of muscle. 'Are you going to send me away from you, without even— saying *adiós*?'

'I should.' His voice shook. 'But—oh God, Leigh—I cannot.'

The discarded towel made a bed for them as, both naked now, they sank on to it, mouths locked, limbs entwined, conscious of nothing but each other, and the shared hunger which so desperately needed assuagement.

Yet by some paradox, there was no longer any need to hurry. They could, she found, linger, prolonging the delicious torment, as his hands and mouth rediscovered the trembling delight of her body.

She felt the tug of his lips on her tumescent breasts, the caress of his fingers against the moist centre of her being, and moaned, softly, aroused beyond words.

Rourke turned suddenly on to his back, lifting her over him, guiding her down to him. She gasped, her eyes dilating as she experienced this new sensation, her eyes questioning as they looked into his, gleaming like Inca gold.

He said huskily, 'I want to watch you, my beautiful one. I want this to remember when you are gone from me.'

Leigh began to move on him, subtly and delicately, discovering to her surprise that she could control their pleasure, in turn enjoying the unrestricted play of his hands worshipping her body. She bent over him, veiling them both in her hair, letting the proud tips of her breasts brush against him, while she kissed the smile that she still thought of as hers alone, her tongue stroking along the curve of his lower lip.

She was aware of the urgency in him mounting until it threatened to overwhelm them both, and abandoned all control, sheer animal instinct taking over. She was all woman, pleasuring her man, her body twisting in a sweet, driving frenzy, shuddering in delight as the first ecstatic spasms of their culmination wrenched her body apart, and flung her headlong into some nameless sunlit void.

Afterwards, they were very quiet together. Rourke held her closely, his lips brushing her half-closed eyelids. Then he led her back into the pool, and washed her gently, drying her on his shirt before helping her back into her clothes as if she had been a child.

You can't send me away, her heart cried out to him. You can't!

But he was no longer smiling, his face absorbed, almost grim as he buttoned her shirt, as if he had already detached himself in spirit as well as physically.

When he had completed his task, he took her hands and raised first one and then the other to his lips in farewell, before turning away.

Leigh said imploringly, 'Rourke. . .' and saw his dark face grow stark.

'No,' he said quietly. 'No, *querida,* don't ask me for what I cannot give.'

She watched him walk away from her. And for the first time thought with pity of the girl from Washington, who had also asked too much.

Leigh stayed by herself for a long time, staring up at the high jagged peaks which closed in the valley, wondering how long it would take her to forget.

She couldn't let herself think about Rourke. It was like pressing on a raw wound to know that, once she left here, she would never see him again.

She turned her mind instead to all the other lesser things that she would miss, which had so swiftly become an integral part of her life.

For the first time in her life, she thought, she had been part of a team, even if her role had been a small and insignificant one. She wanted the Quechua baby she had seen born that morning to grow up strong and well, and she wanted to be there to watch it happen.

She wanted to see Atayahuanco grow and prosper, the small herds of llama and alpaca which Peruvian Quest had brought in to provide subsistence for the Quechua thriving and increasing in number. She wanted to see the flocks' wool woven into the bright traditional ponchos and blankets.

She could, she supposed, come back one day. If essential communications could be radically improved, there were plans once the excavations had been completed to provide some tourist facilities. But it won't be the same, she thought. I'll be a visitor—no longer part of it. And how can I bear it? How can I bear any of it?

She walked back to the camp. As she reached her tent, she heard her name called, and saw Fergus Willard making his way towards her.

'Rourke tells me you're leaving us.' His face was kind, and rather anxious. 'It's entirely for the best, you know. The immediate future is going to be very difficult, very distressing for us all. But Rourke has managed to convince the authorities that you, at least, are completely innocent of any involvement—that you were in total ignorance of Gilchrist's activities.'

She remembered the men who had visited her in Cuzco, the dark, shrewd, considering eyes, and shivered. 'That was—good of him.'

'We shall be sorry to lose you,' he went on, patting her shoulder. 'To be honest, we had misgivings when we heard you planned to come here, but you've fitted in surprisingly well.'

Leigh said steadily, 'That's one of the nicest things anyone's ever said to me.' And meant it. She paused. 'About leaving—if someone could be spared to get me back on to one of the main tourist tracks. . .'

'Oh, there's no question of that.' Fergus sounded almost shocked. He was silent for a moment, his expression tired and rather strained. 'As a matter of fact, a helicopter will be arriving here some time in the next twenty-four hours, and you'll fly down to Cuzco in that—with Gilchrist, I'm afraid, but there's no other way.'

Her lips parted in a soundless gasp. 'You mean—he's really going to be arrested?'

'Yes, it's quite inevitable.' He shook his head. 'I wish you could have been spared this. You being his fiancée, this must be a shattering blow for you. But perhaps you should ask yourself whether a young man so fatally attracted to the prospect of easy money could possibly have made you happy.'

'I think I know the answer to that already.'

He nodded, patted her awkwardly again, and moved off. Leigh went into the tent, and sank down on the edge of her cot, her brain whirling. The police were coming for Evan! It was like a nightmare. A nightmare for which she was partly responsible, because it was due to her that he was at Atayahuanco. If he had stayed in England, other temptations more easily resisted might have come his way, but he wouldn't have been drawn to steal valuable antiquities, she was sure.

She gave a trembling sigh. Well, she had got him into this mess, and she owed it to him to try and get him out. Their love for each other might not have survived their enforced separation, but she couldn't altogether desert him when he needed her. And at Atayahuanco, she was his only friend.

He had vanished before. He could vanish again, she told herself.

She left the tent and strolled as casually as possible towards the men's sleeping quarters. Evan rarely moved far away from his tent these days, not even pretending to play an active part in the project any more.

He was asleep under his mosquito netting when she found him, a luridly jacketed paperback novel face downwards on the floor beside him.

'Evan.' Gently she shook him to wakefulness, and he sat up, blinking blearily at her.

'An unexpected visitor,' he remarked, not altogether pleasantly. 'Is it the pleasure of my company you're after, or are you just sick of playing the little friend to all the world, after all?'

'Neither,' Leigh said curtly, needled by his tone. 'I came to warn you that the police are on their way.'

She saw the colour drain out of his face, leaving a sickly greenish tinge behind. He swayed a little, and for a moment she thought he was going to faint, but he recovered himself.

'What am I going to do?' he whispered. 'Oh, God, what am I going to do?'

'There's only one thing you can do.' She put her hand on his arm. 'You've got to disappear again, into the *puna*. Just as you did before. And you've got to do it fast.'

His sideways glance at her was edgy. 'How the hell can I do that?'

'You managed it quite easily last time.' Leigh kept her voice crisp. 'And you have this tent to yourself, so there's no one overlooking your movements.'

He gave a bark of laughter. 'The camp leper, that's me! But don't think for one moment they're not watching me, because they are—every bloody minute. I'd never get away with a mule this time.'

'Then you'll have to go on foot.' She hesitated. 'I'll—I'll get you some food, and a water bottle. But on one condition.'

'Leigh Frazier, sneak-thief?' He gave her a look of exaggerated admiration. 'My God, you have changed. Well, what's the condition?'

'That you give back what you took. It's the only way, and it may make things easier for you—if—if they catch up with you.'

Evan was silent for a moment. Then, 'Done,' he said smilingly.

'Then give it to me now.'

He laughed again. 'Are you crazy? It's not here. I hid it before I came back, and just as well. Do you know those bastards have actually searched me? And they've been through this tent more than once.' He paused. 'No, darling, we'll swap. My illicit hoard for your food, and whatever money you can scrape together. Is it a deal?'

Leigh nodded. 'In two hours, then.' She tried to speak calmly. 'I'll walk up to the house where we talked this morning. If anyone questions me, I'm going to visit the baby. You'll have to sneak away somehow and meet me there.'

His brows lifted. 'You make a very efficient accomplice, darling. You're full of surprises these days, aren't you?' His eyes narrowed as he studied her. 'No, you're not the girl I tried to romance in England. Not any more.' His smile wasn't pleasant. 'So some lucky swine actually found the key to your chastity belt at last!'

She winced away from his crudity. 'I hardly think that's any of your concern,' she said shortly. She paused. 'Where will you go when you leave here?'

'I think that had better stay my little secret. I do have friends—other contacts I can call on a long way from this exclusive little gathering. You don't have to worry about me.'

'I can't help but worry.' Leigh bit her lip. 'Because it's not just the police you're scared of, is it, Evan?'

He was very still for a moment, and something furtive and ugly looked at her from his eyes. Then he shrugged. 'Someone seems to have been gossiping. But it's no problem. I can look after myself. You see, darling Leigh, I've changed too. I'm not the wimp who used to roll over and beg for favours in England. I know how to protect myself.'

'Then I'm surprised you deign to accept my help,' she returned wearily.

'Oh, I figure you owe me something,' he said casually. 'I was quite looking forward to being Mr Leigh Frazier, after all. Now I'll have to make my own way in the world.'

If she had really loved him, she thought, she would have been stricken to the heart at that admission. As it was, her parting smile held contempt as she turned to leave.

'In two hours, then.'

CHAPTER TEN

IT was not a two hours that Leigh ever wanted to remember.

Evan had called her 'a sneak-thief' and she felt she was wearing the title, emblazoned across her forehead. Part of the trouble was everyone was being so kind, and eager to help her. By now, it seemed to be general knowledge that she was leaving, and the warmth and sympathy being directed towards her were almost tangible, she thought remorsefully. They knew that she and Evan had been engaged, of course. Probably they also knew his arrest was imminent, and thought she was struggling to conceal heartbreak.

If only they knew, she thought guiltily, wearily.

She had no trouble in requisitioning a rucksack and water bottle from the stores, although the provisions were far more of a problem. She couldn't just casually go round helping herself to tins of food, coffee and powdered milk, and it took several trips through the kitchen quarters before she had acquired anything like enough food to keep Evan going even for a couple of days.

She hated herself most for this. No one went hungry at the camp, but the food was fairly strictly rationed, and it seemed dreadful to be robbing the hard working members of the team in order to help Evan escape the consequences of his own folly.

She shivered as she packed the rucksack. No matter how lightheartedly he might have begun his treasure hunt, it was obvious he was now in trouble up to his neck. She wondered how he would fare once he got away from Atayahuanco—where in fact he could go, with the police after him, as well as those other criminal scavengers after the same Inca gold as himself.

She wondered too what Rourke would say when he found out what she had done, and she had no doubt that Evan's escape would be traced back to her. He would be angry, she thought miserably, and with every justification. And it was anguish to think his final memory of her would be as a meddler, interfering with the course of justice.

But if she managed to recover the missing treasures, perhaps that would help to redeem her in Rourke's eyes, she tried to tell herself. He was an archaeologist, after all, and this was his father's country. He clearly cared about its history, as well as its future.

She couldn't bear to think of him reverting to his earlier contemptuous opinion of her—hating her even. But she also knew she would never be able to convince him she felt some kind of responsibility towards Evan.

If only I could see him, talk to him, explain, she thought restlessly.

She was returning to her tent with some freshly baked rolls, when she did see him. He was standing outside the long, low shed where Consuelo cleaned the pottery they found, and painstakingly pieced the fragments together again. Consuelo was with him, and even at a distance of yards, it was evident she was crying.

Leigh felt herself shrinking, mentally as well as physically. There, at least, was one person who would be happy to see her go, she thought.

She wondered why the other girl was so upset. Could it be that she had divined what had happened by the bathing-pool by some female, sexual instinct? Leigh was almost thankful that she couldn't hear what they were saying to each other in such low, urgent voices—thankful that she would soon be miles away, and unable to be hurt any more by the sight of them together. Thankful, too, as Rourke's hands descended on the other girl's shoulders, pulling her towards him, that neither of them had seen her, and she was spared that humiliation at least.

She took another, more roundabout route back to the tent, wretchedly conscious of her purloined bread, waiting every moment to hear someone shouting 'Stop, thief!'

But no one did, and she didn't know whether to be glad or sorry.

She had packed the rucksack, and was wrapping it in one of the blankets she had bought from Maria, when June walked in.

'That's pretty,' June said amiably, flinging herself down on her cot with a heartfelt sigh of relief. 'Did you get it locally?'

'At one of the rest places on the way here.' Leigh could feel hateful colour spreading up to her hairline. 'I—I thought I'd give it to the new baby—as a parting present.'

'That would be a nice thought.' June sounded casually approving, and Leigh breathed more easily. 'Did you see Rourke, by the way? Talk to him about your ex-boyfriend, and his pastimes?'

'I—mentioned it.' She hadn't thought it was possible to blush any more, but it seemed it was. 'He—he won't do anything to help him.'

'Well, you can't blame him for that,' said June sharply. 'In my book, people like Evan Gilchrist are the scum of the earth. Jail's too good for him.'

Leigh looked at her in utter astonishment. In the brief time she had known June, she had felt she had got to know her well, and had always found her tolerant in the extreme, prepared to make allowances for anyone. She had never heard her so vitriolic before.

She said, 'He's weak.'

June snorted. 'Not him! He's a born predator, homing in on other people's weaknesses. If you'd been involved as I've been—seen the results of his activities, and those like him, you wouldn't make excuses for him, believe me.'

Leigh stared at her, bewildered. There was more to this, it was obvious, than an honest person's dislike for a common lawbreaker, she realised. And Rourke wouldn't be the only one to condemn her for helping Evan to escape justice, she thought wretchedly. She was going to forfeit every good opinion she had earned while she was at Atayahuanco. She looked down at the blanket-wrapped rucksack, fighting sudden indecision. She wanted to talk to June— question her, but now there simply wasn't time. If she was going to meet Evan, as they had planned, it had to be now.

She said, 'Well, I'll see you later.'

June grimaced slightly. 'Yes, honey. I didn't mean to sound off like that, but the Evan Gilchrists of the world really turn my stomach. And even if he'd stayed on the right side of the law, you'd still be better off without him.'

Leigh had plenty to think about as she toiled up the steep track towards the citadel. Ahead of her the tumbled masonry shimmered in the heat, dominated by the still imposing structure of the temple of the

Sun. Its elongated shape was like a great stone finger pointing at the sky, she thought, indicating with majesty the great brazen orb it had been built to honour.

She was thankful this part of the excavation was complete, and the team were working now on the other side of the ridge, uncovering what had once been some nobleman's house, or perhaps even the quarters which had housed the retinue of virgins who served the Sun God. It meant there was less likelihood of bumping into anyone who might ask awkward questions.

She paused to catch her breath, and look down on the encampment below. Both Evan and herself had brought them nothing but harm, she thought with compunction. When the police arrived she would have to make it very clear that helping Evan to escape had been her idea, and hers alone.

When she reached the house, the Quechua woman was sitting cross-legged, a baby clamped peacefully to each breast. She greeted Leigh with composed dignity, and seemed genuinely delighted with the gift of the blanket, her impassive face breaking into a smile. In return, Leigh was offered a wad of coca leaves to chew, but, as always, she declined politely, as June and the others had warned her to do.

She had expected to find Evan waiting for her when she emerged once again into the swirling brightness of the street, but he was nowhere to be seen, and she groaned inwardly. She couldn't just hang around, the rucksack and water bottle were too hideously conspicuous for that, so she continued to walk slowly uphill as if she were just out for a stroll, taking a last look round the old fortress town where the Incas had once held sway.

Perhaps Evan hadn't made it, she told herself, trying not to feel too hopeful. Perhaps he had been spotted trying to get away from the camp, and been detained. Was it really possible that she might be let off the hook?'

And discovered almost as soon as that little piece of wishful thinking had formed in her mind that— no, it was not to be that easy.

'Leigh!' Her name was uttered in a loud, husky whisper. She spun round, but apart from a thin dog sleeping in a patch of shadow, the street seemed deserted.

'Leigh!' Definitely Evan's voice, and this time with a hint of impatience. 'Up above you.'

She looked up and saw him, a deeper shadow in the darkness of the temple's entrance.

Picking her way gingerly, she went up the steps which led to its doorway.

'I thought you were never coming.' His eyes were fixed greedily on the rucksack.

She said, 'It wasn't easy.'

'What is?' he shrugged. 'Just give me the food and stuff, and I'll be off. Then you can go back to the camp like a good little girl, and pretend you've never seen me.'

'I don't think I can do that,' she said quietly. 'And you seem to have forgotten something.'

'Well, what is it?' he demanded impatiently. 'I can't hang around here for much longer. Someone's bound to look in on me soon, and realise I've gone. I don't want a hue and cry just yet.'

'The things you stole. You promised you'd give them back.'

'Yes, I did, didn't I?' His tone was reflective. 'I wonder what made me say such a bloody stupid thing. You must have great powers of persuasion, darling.' His tone roughened. 'Now let's drop this nonsense. Give me the food.'

Leigh hugged the rucksack to her. 'Not a chance,' she said. 'Not unless you keep your part of the bargain. Don't you see, Evan, it's the only way.'

'The path of rectitude?' His laugh sounded wild, echoing eerily in the shadows of the temple. 'It's a bit late for that, I'm afraid. And if you think I'm handing over my meal ticket for life, then you're crazy! I've had enough of being a loser—a dogsbody—other people's bloody messenger boy. This time I'm coming out on top!'

Another voice spoke, suddenly, accusingly, making them both jump. 'And what about me? What about my meal ticket? Why didn't you tell me you were leaving?'

There was a hole in the roof, and Consuelo stood spotlighted in the resulting shaft of sunlight, her face angry and suspicious, her dark eyes darting between them.

'What are you doing here with this *puta*?' she demanded aggressively. 'Why do you turn to her, and not to me? We are partners, Evan. You cannot treat me like this!'

Evan was the first to recover himself. 'Were you followed?'

'Of course not. Do you take me for a fool? I saw you leave, but I was the only one.' Consuelo took a step forward. 'What are you doing, *querido?* Where are you going? You cannot leave me here!'

'I'm going to have to, sweetheart.' Evan sounded regretful. 'I'll get the stuff to safety, then I'll send for you—promise.'

'Ay de mi!' Consuelo's voice rose in a wail. 'You cannot do this to me! The police are coming—Martinez has told me so. They know everything—how I

have helped you—about my cousin in Cajamarca. They want to arrest me—to question me. You must take me with you!'

'Don't be silly, angel.' Evan was clearly trying to be soothing, but his tone was ragged at the edges. 'You know that's impossible. And without the stuff, they can't prove a thing. Just stall them for a day or two, then when the fuss dies down, we can be together.'

Consuelo's heavy frown made it clear she found this less than reassuring. She tried another tack. 'What have you told this *gringa?* Why do you concern yourself with her, when you love me, *amado?* Don't you know she is Martinez' woman? I have seen the way she follows him with her eyes, the way he watches her when he thinks no one observes.'

There was a pause, and Evan's eyes narrowed. 'Well, well,' he said silkily. 'That explains a great deal. But you don't have to worry about her, Consuelo. She's been useful, bringing me food, that's all. It's you I care about, and you know it.'

'Then you must take me with you. I am afraid to be here when the police come.' She was beginning to sound hysterical. 'You said we would be together. You did not say I must stay behind. What are you doing to me?'

'Trying to make you see reason.' The reasonable, goodhumoured façade was cracking rapidly. 'For God's sake, Consuelo, don't give me a hard time, *amiga.* You're a clever girl. You can keep the police at bay, long enough for me to get across the border into Colombia. I've got contacts there, who'll shelter me. Then, when it's safe, I'll let you know, and we'll go to Miami together, just as we planned. But for now you must stay here.'

'*No!*' Consuelo almost shrieked the word. '*Madre de Dios,* you have been using me! You are going to abandon me for this rich *gringa*. You want all the money for yourself!'

As she paused for breath, 'And if I do,' Evan said slowly and coldly, 'just what do you think you can do about it?'

She made a noise like an animal in pain, and came at him, eyes blazing, nails raised to tear at him. He sidestepped neatly and hit her a resounding blow to the jaw as her headlong rush faltered. Her head went back under the force of it, then slowly she slumped to the floor.

Leigh found a voice from somewhere. 'You've killed her!' she accused hoarsely.

'No such luck,' he retorted callously. 'She's a tough lady. She'll get over it.'

'But she was in love with you.' In spite of the shock and horror of the last few moments, she could feel joyous relief welling up inside her as she realised just who it had been that Consuelo had been creeping out of the tent to meet each night. It wasn't Rourke, she thought, wanting to laugh and cry at the same time. Oh, it wasn't Rourke!

'Actually, we share a mutual passion for the good things of life, which so far has gone largely unsatisfied. Originally the plan was to split the proceeds three ways with her cousin in Cajamarca, but on second thoughts I think I'd prefer to keep it all to myself. Now give me that bloody food, and I'll be going.'

Leigh clutched the rucksack even more tightly. 'But you can't just leave her like that!'

'Watch me,' he invited, his voice ugly. Then, he paused as if an unwelcome thought had struck him. 'Or are you planning to run down to the camp to get help for her, my embryo Florence Nightingale?'

'Of course. She could be really badly hurt—her jaw broken—anything. . .'

He sighed. 'So much for "he travels fastest who travels alone." Then you, my pet, will just have to come with me. Now I come to think of it, you'd make a useful hostage. The police won't be quite so trigger-happy if they know I've got Justin Frazier's daughter with me. They won't want an international incident.'

'Don't be crazy!' Suddenly, Leigh was afraid of this stranger. Suddenly Rourke's attitude, the remarks June had made, were making a terrible kind of sense. She said, 'It isn't Inca gold, is it, Evan? It's something else.'

He smiled. 'So you've realised at last, have you, ducky? Well, well! No golden apples for my princess, I'm afraid, but a couple of kilos of *pasta basica* which my contacts in Colombia will turn into white gold for me. Your father isn't the only one who knows how to become a millionaire. But my route is slightly more direct.'

Her voice sank to a whisper. 'Through hard drugs? But, Evan, that's evil! You know it is.'

He shrugged. 'I know it's the biggest, richest market in the world. And I'm sick of acting as a courier for the local big boys for peanuts. This time I've put my own deal together.'

'You're obscene!' she gasped.

Evan shrugged. 'As far as I'm concerned, cocaine is just another commodity—with a far higher street value than most. I thought you'd be impressed by my business acumen. But I'd almost forgotten your Puritan streak.' He smiled again. 'Although that's beginning to show some wear and tear, according to Consuelo. So you and the lordly Doctor Martinez have been keeping each other warm during the cold *puna* nights! I could see the Snow Queen had melted for someone at last. It might be—interesting to find out what he's taught you. Perhaps I can add a few points to your curriculum.'

Her blood ran cold. She said, 'I'd rather die than have you touch me.'

His grin was hateful. 'Isn't that what they all say?' His hand moved almost casually, and with utter disbelief Leigh saw he was holding a gun. 'But when it comes down to it, most people cling quite obstinately to life. I don't suppose you'll be any different. Now move,' he added impatiently, as Consuelo began to make small moaning noises.

The sight of the gun made Leigh, absurdly, want to laugh, but some instinct warned her it wouldn't be safe to do so. It was no joke. It was all part of the same nightmare.

Even the intensity of the sunlight couldn't dispel it. Holding her arm, Evan urged her down the temple steps.

He said, 'When Consuelo let me know you were coming to Atayahuanco, I knew I'd be able to turn it to good use. That's why I came back. What I hadn't realised was that they were on to me. I thought I'd be able to spin them some tale which would satisfy them. If you'd done what I wanted and left as soon as you got here, I'd have probably been able to bluff my way through it. But you didn't want to leave, did you, sweetheart?' His voice was savage. 'You wanted to hang round on the offchance of another night of love with that Martinez bastard. That old fool Willard would have been glad to see me go. All he cares about is the reputation of his beloved Peruvian Quest.'

'It didn't occur to you what harm a charge of drug trafficking might do to this kind of project?'

'Do you think I care? I hate this place, and everyone connected with it. And don't let this high moral stance by the authorities fool you. It suits them to let the Indians grow *coca,* and chew it, because it keeps them biddable. So why shouldn't they sell their crop instead and have some fun out of life, instead of stumbling around half-dazed most of the time?'

She said, 'I'm not going to debate the merits of *coca* with you, Evan. It's been around for so long, I doubt whether the government could ban its use if they tried. All I know is that what you're doing is not only illegal, but wicked. And if I'd known. . .'

'Ah, but you didn't.' They were climbing now, so rapidly it made Leigh's head swim. 'And if it hadn't been for Rourke Martinez and his interference, I could probably have persuaded you to take my package to Lima with you. It might even have gone back to Britain in some diplomatic bag—I'm sure your father will have contacts at the Embassy you could have used.'

'You like to use everyone, don't you, Evan?' She tried to keep her voice level, the disgust under control, because she couldn't count on his stability any more.

Had he always been like this, she wondered, with herself too blind to see it? Or had some chance exposure to the fringes of the drug trade been the black alchemy which had changed him?

She said, 'We'll have to slow down. I can't keep up this pace. . .'

'You're going to have to. I want to put as great a distance between us and the camp as possible before it gets dark.' His hand closed brutally on her arm, and she had to choke back a cry. 'So don't slow me down, sweetie, or you'll regret it.'

She said, 'But you can't hope to get away with it. You've admitted yourself that it's not just the police looking for you.' She remembered what Rourke had said, and shuddered. 'And now there's Consuelo, and this cousin of hers. They won't like being double-crossed.'

'Juan won't know, until it's too late for him to do anything about it. And Consuelo is too scared of prison to say very much. If she's got any sense she'll make herself out as the brave heroine who tried to stop the wicked drug-smuggler from making a run for it. She'll have a bruise the size of an egg to back her story up, so she should be grateful to me.'

'Grateful? Evan, she's in love with you!'

'That's her tough luck.' His tone was dismissive. 'She's nearly seven years older than me, for God's sake. What did she expect? She was a virgin too,' he added musingly. 'But unlike you, she couldn't wait to get rid of hers. It was while we were in bed together that she started telling me about her cousin who worked for one of the big bad drug barons. No wonder all the Secret Services think pillow talk's so dangerous! Eventually I got to meet Juan, and to show good faith I managed to get a couple of consignments taken out on the supply helicopter. And so—a star was born.'

Leigh said in a low voice, 'I don't want to hear about it.'

He laughed. 'Just making conversation. Or would you rather talk about the might-have-beens, when I was a starry-eyed innocent trying to marry into money?'

She winced. 'Was that all it was?'

'I suppose I loved you,' he said after a pause. 'I know I fancied you like hell, you frigid little bitch. But I'm afraid, like some wines, my passion didn't travel very well. Within a month of getting here, I was so pigged off with Atayahuanco and everything to do with it, I could hardly remember what you looked like. And by that time, Consuelo was making welcoming sounds.' He gave her arm a cruel jerk. 'Come on, darling. Another mile, and this bloody valley will be behind us for ever.' He smiled. 'And then it will be you and me against the world—just as you always wanted, won't that be nice?'

It was an hour and a half later when they stopped for the first time. Leigh sat, her back against a boulder, her heart hammering, and her lungs feeling they were about to burst. They were on a high ridge, overlooking a valley, the almost precipitous sides of which descended to a small, dark lake. It was degrees colder up here, and Leigh shivered, hugging her arms defensively round her body.

She was looking at a curiously shaped cairn of stones, erected long before the conquest to propitiate some savage local deity. At its foot, Evan was digging busily. From his muttered recognition of various landmarks along the way, and his air of supreme self-satisfaction, Leigh guessed he had found his cache.

His back was turned to her, and if ever there was a moment to run, it was then, but she didn't have the strength. Besides, there was little shelter on the ridge—and he did have the gun, and she had no illusions that she could outrun that.

Through half-closed eyes she saw a sudden movement, and looking up, her heart skipping a beat, hoping against hope that it was the promised helicopter combing the mountains for them. But, of course, she would have heard a helicopter.

The flight she was witnessing had a silent, powerful grace that no machine could hope to emulate.

'What are you staring at?' Evan was wiping the dirt from two polythene-wrapped packages, and looking at her sourly.

She pointed. 'There's a condor.'

'Big deal,' he said. 'It's only a bloody vulture, you know.'

Leigh shook her head. 'No, it's a magic bird.' Her mind went back to that night—the night of the condor, and she rehearsed the chant in her head until she could sing it aloud. '*O condorcito.*'

Even in daylight, it had a haunting, eerie sound, and it disturbed him, she could tell.

He said roughly, 'Are you out of your mind—singing to a damned bird?'

She said, 'It's a good omen.'

'It's ridiculous superstition.' She'd caught him off balance for the first time. 'You want to watch it, Leigh, or you'll end up going native, prancing round in a poncho, and a black hat with a baby tied to your back.'

She got to her feet, dusting off her jeans. 'I can think of worse fates,' she said calmly. As the huge bird swept in a wide circle above her head, she sent a silent prayer up to it. '*Condorcito,* you brought us together through your magic. Tell him where I am. Send him to find me.'

'That's enough bird-watching.' Evan was stowing his packages in the rucksack, before hoisting it on to his shoulder. 'Let's get going. We have still quite a distance to cover before nightfall.'

He was right, she thought, as they set off. It was superstition. But all the same, her glimpse of the condor had been absurdly comforting, and she craned her neck to watch it until it was out of sight.

As the sun began to go down, Evan's temper seemed to deteriorate with it. He was clearly regretting having brought her with him, and this frightened Leigh. How long would it be, she wondered, before he decided to abandon her on the *puna,* and would she be alive or dead when he did so?'

Their pace had slowed considerably, to her relief, and he seemed on edge, constantly scanning the sky, and the slopes of neighbouring peaks.

He stopped suddenly more than once, demanding, 'Do you hear anything?'

'No.' It was the truth, but she was beginning to share his unease. The sense that they were not alone, and that unseen eyes were plotting their progress was an overwhelming one.

She thought hopefully, Rourke? but there was no answering lift in her heart, or warm stir in her blood. And soon it would be dark. . .

They were traversing with care the edge of a small tree-lined canyon when Evan pointed suddenly. 'Down there. Isn't that a roof?'

'I think it is.' Leigh peered uncertainly in the direction indicated. 'But how do we get down there?'

Almost before the words were spoken, she heard a noise like the distant crack of a whip and saw Evan stagger suddenly, his face wearing an expression of almost ludicrous surprise. He half turned to her as if he was going to speak and, incredulously, Leigh saw the crimson stain spreading on the front of his shirt. He was falling towards her, and she tried to get out of the way, only to feel the ground at the edge crumbling under her weight, then giving way completely. She gave one wild, terrified scream, then she was lost and falling, dried bushes and protruding roots tearing at her clothes and skin as she slid helplessly downwards.

Her descent was brought to an abrupt and bone-shaking halt. For a moment she lay, her eyes closed, her arms wrapped round her head to protect herself from the shower of earth and loose stones still raining down in her wake. Then that too stopped, and everything was still.

Leigh was still too, breathing quietly, amazed to find she still could. She began to test herself, moving each limb in turn to make sure nothing was broken or sprained. Then she lifted her head slowly and looked round. She was a mess, and she hurt all over, but she was intact, lying, as far as she could judge, on a narrow ledge.

There was no sign of Evan, but just to the left of her refuge, the bushes and stunted shrubs had been torn away as if something heavy had forced a passage down into the canyon.

She shuddered. But it didn't have to be Evan, she told herself. Perhaps he hadn't fallen into the canyon at all, but was lying, wounded, on the edge.

And as if to justify that belief, she heard the sound of movement above her. She was about to call out his name, when something—some sixth sense—kept her quiet, huddled against the rock face so that she was sheltered by the remaining bushes as well as the slight overhang.

Because it couldn't be Evan, she realised as nausea rose in her throat. Evan had been shot, and he was dead. She knew that now, although she had never seen anyone die before. She remembered the soundlessly moving mouth, the oddly blank eyes, and her whole body clenched in panic.

There was a presence above her—she couldn't gauge it more accurately than that—and she sensed it looking down. Looking for signs of life, she thought, her throat working convulsively. It was the anonymous presence she had sensed earlier. The presence which had dogged their footsteps, which had killed Evan, and had come to make sure of her, to verify the evidence of her scream and fall.

She was entirely motionless, controlling her ragged breathing in quiet desperation.

Silence seemed to wrap them both round, bonding them in a weird intimacy—Leigh, hiding on her ledge, and Evan's killer who wanted her dead too. It seemed endless.

At last she heard voices, a brief snatch of a conversation in Spanish which she vainly strained her ears, trying to comprehend.

Then, as if the sun had emerged from behind a cloud of darkness, the presence was gone. She was alone.

She didn't move for a while, hardly daring to believe her luck, telling herself it might be a bluff to coax her into the open. It was only when she sat up and took proper stock of her situation that she realised how foolish she was being.

The ledge, it seemed, was as far as she went. She got slowly to her knees, and then to her feet, reaching up wincing to the nearest clump of foliage and testing its strength, only to feel the shallow roots pull away in her hand.

To get up to the edge, she would need to climb, but the canyon face was too unstable to tackle without proper handholds. Or there was down.

She took a swift look, then shuddered, assailed by sudden giddiness. Below her was a sheer drop into the trees.

Rule One, she told herself shakily, was under no circumstances to look down. She checked each side of her, verifying what she already knew—that after the ledge she was occupying petered out, there was no other refuge.

It was a miracle that her fall had taken her over the edge at the only place where it could be broken, or so she had thought. Now she was beginning to think again. The ledge might not be a refuge after all, but a trap, from which she could move neither up nor down.

It came to her, chillingly, that she might come to wish she had fallen all the way and been killed outright.

The sun was almost down. Soon, too soon, it would be dark, and cold. She was shivering already with shock and fear, her teeth chattering. She would also soon be hungry and thirsty. She had no covering apart from her torn clothes, no food, and nothing to drink.

She drew her knees up to her chin, and wrapped her arms round them, trying to make herself as small as possible to conserve her body heat. She wouldn't, she told herself, even think about the clamour of empty stomach and dry throat. One problem at a time was enough.

If she took off one of her boots, she wondered if she could knock some hand and footholds in the steep canyon face with her heel, and scramble up that way. She swallowed. It was a forlorn hope, especially when the light was fading rapidly, and although she regarded herself as reasonably athletic, she had no actual climbing experience at all.

She sensed another movement, and shrank, biting back a terrified cry, only to discover it was the condor, swirling above the treetops in a wide dignified sweep.

It was a relief to see another living creature, she thought, rubbing her eyes wearily with the back of her hand, even though Evan had called it a vulture. Had it scented carrion—and was that why it was circling round the canyon now? The thought made her swallow sickly.

She thought shakily, If ever I needed magic, I need it now. *O condorcito!*

The next hour passed with agonising slowness. Apart from the physical discomfort of her scratches and grazes, Leigh was growing cramped and tired on the narrow ledge. She supposed if she lay down with care, she could sleep, but what would happen if she turned over in her sleep made her blood run cold. She would have to try and stay awake, she thought, altering her position slightly and painfully.

Then she tensed with disbelief as she heard voices. Oh God, surely it wasn't true! Surely Evan's killers hadn't returned yet again. She was paralysed with fright, unable this time even to draw herself back into the shelter of the overhang. If they looked down, shone a light, they would see her, and there was nothing she could do about it.

And then she heard her name called, hoarsely, desperately—as he had shouted it that day when she was nearly swept away in the river, she remembered. She licked her dry lips, trying to force her recalcitrant throat muscles to work, but she could only manage an answering croak. 'Rourke?'

'Querida!' No one had ever invested that word with so much feeling, she thought, staring up into the gathering darkness. She could see lights, so he was not alone. *'Querida,* where are you?'

'On a ledge, but I can't climb up. Everything just—gives way.'

Including herself, she recognised. She was near to tears suddenly, trembling as weakly as a newborn kitten.

'I'm climbing down.'

'No—it's not safe. You'll fall!'

'I have a rope. Keep still, *mi amada*.' Eternity passed then she heard the sound of scraping and slithering, and he was beside her. 'Are you hurt?' His hands touched her gently. 'Can you stand?'

'I think so,' she whispered, but she wasn't sure, and she was grateful when he lifted her with infinite care, holding her against him as he fastened the rope round her.

'Don't try to climb, or do anything. You'll be pulled up.'

'Yes.' There were tears mingling with the blood and grime on her face. I must look hideous, she thought. 'I'm sorry. It—it was my fault. . .'

'Hush, *amiga*.' He tucked her hair back behind her ears, the simple movement a caress. 'We'll talk about it later. Now, up you go.'

Leigh had no idea who was at the other end of the rope, but they pulled her up as if she had been a featherweight, and there were hands at the end to pull her over the edge to safety. She collapsed on to her knees, the breath sobbing in her lungs as she looked round the circle of light at the faces surrounding her. Some she recognised instantly—Fergus Willard for one, and Jim Holloway who led the medical team. And the policeman with the moustache and the sad eyes. She tried to tell him she was sorry too, but no sound would come.

And then she saw the tall man pushing his way through the group, the rather harsh features twisted with concern.

'Leigh!' he exclaimed. 'My darling child, what's happened to you?'

He voice cracked. 'Daddy?' Then the lights went out, and the darkness swallowed her up.

CHAPTER ELEVEN

THE view from the hotel bedroom window was as spectacular as she had once surmised, but Leigh looked down on it with eyes that saw nothing but the bleakness of her own inner world.

Behind her, in the bedroom, she could hear swift efficient movements as one of the chambermaids packed for her, on her father's instructions. He was in his own suite, presumably finalising the arrangements for their flight back to the United Kingdom.

Leigh sighed soundlessly. A week had passed since she had been hauled bodily up the face of the canyon. A week during which a great deal had happened.

In spite of her protests she had been taken back to Atayahuanco on a stretcher, and flown the next day to a private clinic in Cuzco for a complete medical check-up. Apart from infection, Leigh knew that Justin Frazier had feared pneumonia from shock, but his worries had proved groundless.

'I'm tougher than I look,' she had told him over and over again, and at last he had reluctantly accepted that her claim might have some truth.

She had been interviewed by Pedro Morales, who had been more understanding than she deserved. He had confirmed what her father refused to discuss—that Evan's body had been found at the base of the canyon, with the rucksack nearby. Leigh had wept a little then, rather for what Evan had once been to her than for what he had become. Wept for the waste, and the pity of it all. His parents, she knew, were dead, but he had an older sister married with a family.

'Do they—need to know the truth?' she had asked haltingly.

'By no means, *señorita*. They can be told there has been a climbing accident.'

She was content with that.

Justin Frazier came to visit her each day, his presence an invigoration in itself.

He, of course, knew everything, and he made it clear Leigh's halting explanations were unnecessary.

'They shouldn't have sent for you,' she had protested tearfully at the beginning.

'Nonsense,' he had said robustly. 'You're my only child, Leigh, and even if you are behaving like a complete fool, as long as I live I'll be there for you.'

He told her too all the things she was still in the dark about.

'My arrival was a blessing,' he said matter-of-factly. 'Because when the radio message came through to the camp advising I was on the helicopter with Morales and the police contingent, Martinez went to look for you up at the citadel—and there of course was that unfortunate young woman, who was able to tell him exactly what had happened.'

'Poor Consuelo! Is—is she all right.'

Justin Frazier shrugged. 'She's helping the police with their enquiries, and she'll have to face charges,' he said shortly. 'But Morales himself admits that they're only on the fringes of the drug-trafficking—she and this cousin of hers. But they may get some lead to guide them towards the big boys.'

'Who shot Evan?' she asked in a subdued voice.

'As easily as you or I might swat a fly, my dear. It seems they'd begun using him as a courier—a mere pawn in their activities—and when he cheated and robbed them, it couldn't be allowed to go unpunished.' He looked at her gravely. 'It would have been better if he'd stayed in the camp, and waited for the police to come for him, Leigh.'

'I know—I see that now.' The tears were scalding her cheeks. 'But—he was so scared—of prison.'

Her father sighed swiftly. 'Then perhaps it was for the best. Who can say?' He patted her hand. 'Now rest, darling, and get those grazes healed so I can take you home.'

The question she wanted to ask but dared not was, 'Where's Rourke?'

She had been aware of him on the trip back to Atayahuanco, before Jim Holloway's sedative took effect. But he wasn't there when the helicopter took off, and although she had waited with painful eagerness each day at the clinic in Cuzco, he hadn't appeared.

She tried to tell herself she hadn't imagined the tenderness she had heard in his voice, sensed in his hands during those brief moments on the ledge, but as the empty days passed she began to wonder if he hadn't simply been showing her the kind of reassurance he would have shown a panicking child, or a frightened animal—soothing her to make things easier for her rescuers, to make their task easier.

Now, she and her father were back in Lima, and the following day they would be flying out. And still no word from him.

She couldn't avoid the thought that he was punishing her for helping Evan to run away in the first instance, although he must surely know that she had suffered enough.

'*Don't ask*,' he had warned, '*for what I cannot give*.'

Leigh sighed, turning away from the window. He had given, of course; she could not deny that. He had needled her into a courage she hadn't known she possessed. He had shown her new horizons. He had shared with her, briefly, a warmth and passion beyond her wildest dreams.

If she had wanted more, then that was her problem, not his. He had promised nothing.

Perhaps he had been intuitive enough to guess what she was feeling, and had decided that a clean break was the kindest way to end it, without difficult explanations and confrontations.

She had once ventured to ask how the search party had happened on the right place.

'Apparently Gilchrist had left a trail a child could follow,' Justin Frazier had said dismissively. 'But Martinez seems to have a genius for that kind of thing. Although at one time I wondered if that damned altitude sickness one hears about had got to him,' he added frowningly. 'Kept ranting on about some blasted great bird—convinced that if we followed it, we'd find you.'

'Ah,' Leigh had said quietly, her heart doing a great tumultuous somersault for joy. The magic, at least, had been real for both of them. She   that to treasure always.

There was a knock at the door of the suite, and she glanced at her watch. She supposed it would be tea arriving. Justin Frazier had arranged the little ritual each day, and always came to have tea with her.

She smiled rather sadly as she crossed to the door. Poor Daddy! He was so determined to restore normality to her life as soon as possible, even in small ways like this.

She opened the door, and stood motionless, feeling the colour drain out of her face.

'You seem surprised to see me,' Rourke said quietly. He walked past her into the suite, dropping his jacket carelessly on to the nearest chair. The chambermaid appeared in the bedroom doorway, obviously agog at the sight of him, and he reached into a pocket and gave her some money, adding a few succinct words in Spanish which had her scuttling for the door.

When they were alone, he gave Leigh a narrow-eyed, comprehensive assessment from head to toe. 'You look better,' he commented. 'Have all your bruises healed?'

'Most of them.' She looked back at him, transparent as glass, unable any longer to conceal what she felt, and not caring either.

He groaned softly. 'Leigh, I came here to talk rationally to you, *querida*, but when you look at me like that, all I can think of is how long it is since I held you in my arms.'

Once in a different lifetime, he had picked her up in his arms and carried her through to this very bedroom, put her down on this very bed, and lain beside her, just as he was doing now. She had thought she hated him then, but she hadn't been able to deny the excitement his touch had engendered. And now she didn't have to deny it.

As he reached for her, she surrendered eagerly, her mouth seeking his. If this was to be their last goodbye, then it would be a memorable one, she thought deliriously as her lips parted for him.

Rourke kissed her as if he would drain her to the depths of her soul, as if the parting of the last few days had been as great a torment for him as for her.

Then he held her, tightly, closely, wrapping her in his arms as if he would never let her go.

He said huskily, 'I thought I'd lost you. *Dios*, Leigh, if you know what I went through, knowing you were with him—knowing the danger you were in!' He kissed her eyes. 'Once before, in the river, you were nearly snatched from me. It will not happen a third time.'

She said, 'I don't understand. . .'

'I cannot live without you, *querida*. Nor will I. Tell me it is the same for you. Tell me you will marry me.'

'You want me?' She couldn't believe it. 'You really want me—like that?'

'In all the ways there are, my Leigh.'

'Why didn't you tell me before—why didn't you let me know? I was so unhappy. . .'

He sighed. 'Because I promised your father I would give you some time—to recover mentally as well as physically from what had happened to you. And although I have given Fergus my resignation from the Atayahuanco project, I could not leave him to deal with the police enquiries unaided, and so. . .'

'You've done what?' Leigh was no longer lying pliantly in his arms, but sitting upright staring down at him.

He lifted himself on to one elbow, his brows raised in surprise. 'I have resigned,' he said matter-of-factly. 'Your father is, of course, perfectly correct. The project is no life for a woman, as he made clear when I told him I wanted to marry you.'

'When did you tell him this?'

'Your last day at Cuzco. I had flown down with Morales. You were asleep, but I sat with you, and knew that whatever the cost, I could not let you go.'

She said stupidly, 'But the project is your life—everyone knows that.'

Rourke shook his head, his eyes holding hers steadily. 'You are my life, *querida*. Without you there is darkness and emptiness.'

'But Isabella—you didn't marry her because she hated it at Atayahuanco.'

He sighed. 'I didn't marry Isabella, *mi amada*, because we were totally unsuited to each other. We enjoyed a glamorous relationship, all parties and candlelit dinners. It was not destined to survive the kind of reality Atayahuanco provides.'

'And you thought I wouldn't survive it either,' she said huskily.

Rourke nodded. 'That's true. I thought you were another social butterfly, even more pampered than Isabella.' He grinned. 'But first, I found a shrew. Then a would-be siren, whose lips told me a very different story. Then a stubborn, pigheaded little fool,' he added a mite grimly.

'Well, thank you so much.' She lay back on the pillows, watching him under her lashes. 'And when did you begin to change your mind?'

His grin widened. 'Who says I have?' he asked unforgivably, dodging laughingly the punch she aimed at him, and capturing her clenched fist to kiss it. 'I began to change my mind, *querida*, when you were so gallant about the contents of Maria's stew. And it disturbed me to find, also, that I could not rid my mind of how you had felt in my arms. I had started to make love to you that night to teach you a lesson, yet in the end I was the one who was punished. I spent the rest of the night fighting the kind of fantasies I haven't had since adolescence, imagining you hadn't pushed me away, and that you were there in bed with me, naked and beautiful and willing. I began to think I would never sleep again.'

Leigh said slowly, 'But it was her name you spoke—that morning in the tent.'

His mouth twisted wryly. 'I'm sorry, *querida*, but our relationship wasn't just glamorous—it was also—very physical. My dreams that night had been a little confused.'

She said, 'I suppose I can forgive you. After all, I was a little confused myself for a while.'

'I know.' He stroked her hair back from her face. 'I was so afraid for you, my darling, so terrified that you were going to be hurt. I wanted to protect you from the knowledge of what Gilchrist had done, but it was impossible. And when I heard he had come back to the camp, I was in agony.'

'But you must have known I wasn't in love with him any more,' she protested. A slight flush rose in her face. 'I thought I'd proved that quite conclusively.'

'Because of one night?' Rourke shook his head. 'For all I knew, you might have been carried away by the magic of the condor dance into some brief madness. After all, up to then you'd talked of little else but being reunited with Gilchrist.' His face grew sombre. 'As well as loathing him for his drug-running activities, I then had to cope with being furiously jealous of him. After all, it was him and not me you were engaged to. I had no real claim at all, whereas he had the right to touch and kiss you—even though he'd been having an affair with Consuelo Estebán almost since his arrival on the project.'

'And I thought she was in love with you,' Leigh said ruefully.

He looked at her in amazement. 'How could you have believed such a thing?'

'I was jealous too—and miserable.' She swallowed. 'You see, Greg had told me about Isabella, and how the project always came first with you. And he implied that you only went in for casual affairs.'

'Was it a casual affair when I gave you my ring?' The topaz eyes were very tender.

'No—at least, I didn't think so. But when you took your ring back, I didn't know what to think. Why did you?'

'Because in the cold light of day, I felt I'd made a fool of myself,' Rourke admitted. 'However much I might hate the idea, your engagement to Gilchrist was still a fact. I had to come to terms with the fact that I might just have been a casual affair to you.' He paused. 'And at the camp, you seemed to avoid me.'

She carried his hand to her cheek. 'It was you avoiding me,' she accused tenderly.

'What did you expect me to do? Treat you as an acquaintance when I wanted to tell the whole world you belonged to me?' He shook his head again. 'And I was so proud of you—so proud of the way you adjusted—took the camp and the valley in your stride, and made yourself part of it. And yet at the same time, I wished you a thousand miles away—safe from Gilchrist and his criminal intrigues. I thought when you found out what he was really doing, you would turn from him in disgust. But you never did.'

'Because I didn't know.' She sighed. 'I was so fixated on this treasure hunt he'd once talked about that I couldn't think of anything else. And no one actually mentioned drugs. If Consuelo hadn't followed us to the temple that day, I might still be in the dark.'

'In a way, she is to be pitied,' Rourke said quietly. 'She was infatuated with him. Up to that time, she had been a good worker—an expert member of the team. It seems it was a chance remark that revealed to Gilchrist her cousin was marginally involved in the cocaine trade. He persuaded her to introduce them—and it all began.'

'And now it's ended,' said Leigh in a low voice.

'For some it is. For us, *querida*, there is another beginning—if that is what you want. You have not yet told me that you will marry me.'

She twined her arms round his neck. 'I'd marry you tomorrow if it were possible. Or preferably tonight,' she added thoughtfully.

Rourke kissed her. 'That would be my preference too,' he whispered. 'But there are unfortunate formalities which must be observed. However,' with studied casualness, he began to unfasten the tiny buttons of her silk shirt, 'there is no reason why we should not—rehearse a little.'

She captured his straying fingers. 'But first there's something we have to settle.'

'Settlements?' His brows lifted. 'But surely that is something my father should discuss with yours?'

She was momentarily diverted. 'Of course—I'd forgotten I was marrying money. But that isn't what I meant. Rourke, you have to withdraw your resignation from Peruvian Quest, or—or I won't marry you.'

There was a silence. Then, 'You're crazy,' he said slowly. '*Dios*, Leigh, you've been there—you know what it's like. As a novelty, perhaps you could stand it, but to live there day in, day out for months at a time—no, I couldn't ask it of you.'

'But you didn't ask me,' she said simply. 'Darling Rourke, I know what I mean to you now, but I would never ask you to make such a sacrifice. If being with you means living at Atayahuanco, then that's where I'll be. After all, the project's just beginning to take off. They need you.'

He cupped her face between his hands. 'And I need you,' he assured her unsteadily. 'And it is you who would be making the sacrifice.'

'Then I make it gladly. Now, promise me you'll radio Doctor Willard tomorrow and tell him you're coming back.'

'But only for a limited period.' His tone brooked no argument. 'I want children from you, my wife, and a proper home with you. Nothing can mean more than that.'

'Oh, we'll argue the precise details another time.' Demurely Legh replaced his hand in the vicinity of her shirt buttons. 'Now, where were we?'

He frowned. 'I have a terrible memory.'

'Then I'll have to jog it for you.' Her own hand was straying with delicate sensuality to do just that, when she sat bolt upright with a gasp. 'My God, Daddy!'

'I don't see him.' Rourke undid several more buttons.

'I mean he'll be here any minute for tea.' She saw he was shaking his head. 'Darling, I mean it. He has tea with me here each day around this time.'

'But not today.' Gently, Rourke slid the shirt from her shoulders. 'I told him I wanted to be alone with you.'

'And he agreed?' asked Leigh faintly, amazement that her formidable father should meekly accept instructions from his future son-in-law warring with the havoc that his fingers, stroking her bare skin, were wreaking.

'Of course. So we shall not be interrupted.' The clasp of her bra proved no opposition for him whatever. 'Unless you'd prefer to have tea?'

'I'd prefer to have you,' she said unevenly.

'And so you shall, *querida,* for as long as we both live.' He removed his signet ring and once more put it on her finger. 'Whatever ceremony we go through is for our families. This, my love, my life, is our real wedding.'

'Yes,' Leigh said with a little sigh. 'Oh, yes!' And after that she said nothing more for a very long time.

Six exciting series for you every month... from Harlequin

Harlequin Romance·
The series that started it all

Tender, captivating and heartwarming...
love stories that sweep you off to faraway places
and delight you with the magic of love.

◆

Harlequin Presents·
Powerful contemporary love stories...as individual as the women who read them

The No. 1 romance series...
exciting love stories for you, the woman of today...
a rare blend of passion and dramatic realism.

◆

Harlequin Superromance®
It's more than romance... it's Harlequin Superromance

A sophisticated, contemporary romance-fiction
series, providing you with a longer,
more involving read...a richer mix of complex plots,
realism and adventure.

Harlequin
American Romance™
Harlequin celebrates the American woman...

...by offering you romance stories written about American women, by American women for American women. This series offers you contemporary romances uniquely North American in flavor and appeal.

◆

Harlequin Temptation™
Passionate stories for today's woman

An exciting series of sensual, mature stories of love...dilemmas, choices, resolutions... all contemporary issues dealt with in a true-to-life fashion by some of your favorite authors.

◆

Harlequin Intrigue
Because romance can be quite an adventure

Harlequin Intrigue, an innovative series that blends the romance you expect... with the unexpected. Each story has an added element of intrigue that provides a new twist to the Harlequin tradition of romance excellence.

Harlequin Books

PROD-A-2